Knockouts
Series editor: Josie Levine

A Taste of Freedom

This strange new feeling
Ras is thought a fool by the white carpenter who hires him. But Ras guards his silence, watching, listening. He escapes – and returns in a strange mood.

Where the sun lives
Maria's future looks bleak, even though her cruel and callous Mistress is dying. Until, early one morning, she sees 'a man riding, slow and quiet,' a man who knows where the sun lives.

Christmas love story
William and Ellen Craft attempt a bold and nerve-racking journey to escape from slavery.

Also available in Knockouts:

A Taste of Freedom
Three stories
from black history

Julius Lester

Longman

LONGMAN GROUP LIMITED
Longman House
Burnt Mill, Harlow, Essex CM20 2JE, England
and Associated Companies throughout the World.

© Julius Lester 1983

First published 1983
ISBN 0 582 25052 8 (cased)
     0 582 20128 4 (paper)

Set in 12/15pt Monophoto Times New Roman

Printed in Hong Kong
by Wilture Enterprises (International) Ltd.

Contents

for
Elena Milad and Davis Julius

This strange new feeling

Jakes Brown didn't know what to think that July morning when he saw the young black man waiting by the toolshed for him. He saw a big man, with muscles like ropes bulging from his torn and dirty cotton shirt. He was Jakes' height, five feet nine inches, and weighed one hundred and eighty pounds, at least. But his shoulders were rounded, and his back had a slight stoop to it, as if he were an old man. In those torn pants, which barely covered his knees, and the sleeveless shirt, he looked like a stuffed and weathered scarecrow.

The young white man introduced himself.

'My name's Jakes Brown,' he said, holding out his hand and smiling.

'Yes, sir,' the black man responded in a monotone, staring at the ground.

Jakes felt foolish with his hand extended and after a moment, let it drop.

'What do I call you?' he asked, determined to be friendly.

'Ras.'

'Ras what?'

'Ras, sir,' he said, still staring at the ground.

Jakes wondered if he had been given the dumbest slave on the plantation for a helper. Ras? What kind of name was that? A man had to have two names, or at least one that made sense. Ras!

Jakes took a key from his pocket and unlocked the shed. Well, what did it matter to him? All he wanted was to finish the job, collect his pay and get back home to Maine.

'You know where the tobacco shed is, Ras?'

'Yes, sir.'

'Well, you're going to help me build another one right beside it.'

'Yes, sir.'

'Call me Jakes. Everybody does.'

'Yes, sir.'

'Didn't you understand me?' Jakes flared, irritated with the dull response.

'Yes, sir.'

'Aw, forget it!' he exploded. 'Bring them tools and sawhorses over to the shed. When you finish that, you can start carrying that lumber stacked behind the toolshed.'

'Yes, sir.'

Jakes walked away angrily, sorry now that he had decided to come South for the summer. But he'd heard that work was plentiful during the summer, and that the wages were good. He was young, strong, and had thought it would be fun to do something different. It would give him some good stories to tell through the long, cold winter. But nobody would believe there could be a creature as dumb as Ras. And after you said he was dumb, there was nothing more to tell.

All morning Ras carried tools and lumber, understanding now why Master Lindsay had had them clear new ground last fall and plant more tobacco than ever this spring. Ras' shoulders still ached thinking about the chilly mornings, fog lying over the ground like scraps of cotton, as he and Uncle Isaac cleared the woods on the other side of the field. He smiled, remembering how he had made that double-headed axe ring against the trees until they had trembled, swayed and then fallen – as slowly as a large hawk alighting on a branch. Ras supposed he and Uncle Isaac had cleared fifteen acres by themselves.

His shoulders ached, too, remembering how he and the other slaves had worked through the winter to prepare the newly-cleared ground

3

for planting. He hated that the most – burning the cut trees, and smelling of smoke and ashes for weeks afterward. Then he and the other slaves spread the ashes over the field, raking and pounding the ashes into the soil until the field was almost as fine as dirt. Now he was going to help build the new barn where the tobacco would hang until it was cured.

Ras wondered sometimes if he would have rather been a mule. Coming in from the fields at evening, he would stop at the corral and look at the mules inside. He supposed there were some differences between him and them. But the differences seemed to be to the mules' advantage. They had four legs to his two. When it rained or was chilly, they stayed in the barn. They had as much to eat as they wanted. Ras couldn't remember Master Lindsay ever selling a mule, either.

He didn't know how old he was when Master Lindsay sold his mother. Aunt Jessie had told him how he cried and cried when he came in from the field to find his mother gone.

'You was a little fella, then,' Aunt Jessie had said. 'It was your first summer in the fields. You had to pick the worms off the tobacco leaves.'

Ras remembered. He remembered, too, that

Aunt Jessie and Uncle Isaac had taken him to their cabin and spread straw in a corner for him to sleep on. Time passed, and one day he cried because he couldn't remember what his mother looked like. And more time passed. One day, when he tried to remember her voice, it was gone, too, and Aunt Jessie had died by then, and couldn't put her arms around him and tell him, 'It's all right, child,' even though she didn't know what was wrong. Finally, the day came when nothing remained except a name – Mother – and he didn't know what that was.

A mule didn't need to remember its mother. A mule didn't know it had ever had one. Once, Ras imagined himself asking one of the mules to exchange places with him. He knew that the mule hadn't answered, but he swore he heard a voice say, 'A mule has got more sense than to want to be a slave.'

In the evenings, Ras sat on the steps of the cabin he shared with Uncle Isaac in the slave quarters. The twenty cabins were lined in two rows facing each other, a dusty clearing stretching between. They were built of cheap lumber or logs and had no windows. But the cracks between the boards and logs allowed in light, and in the winter, the cold. Each cabin was a small, dark room with a fireplace for cooking. Those who knew how, built chairs and tables. They were few. No one had beds. They slept on boards and covered themselves with the thin blanket Master Lindsay gave each slave at Christmas. A blanket never lasted the winter.

Ras watched the slaves as they returned from the fields, talking quietly as they went wearily to their cabins. He had already eaten his supper of cornmeal cakes and a strip of bacon. If he had worked in the fields that day, instead of with the white carpenter, he might have gone to sleep without troubling to build a fire, grind the corn into meal, mix it with water, and put the dough on the hot coals to cook.

The sight of Sally walking slowly toward him stopped his remembering. He wanted to get up and go in the cabin, but couldn't because she had seen him. So he remained on the step, enduring the strange discomfort that overcame him whenever he saw her. At least, working with the carpenter, he didn't have to be around her all day anymore, afraid to speak to her and more afraid when she spoke to him.

'Evening, Ras.'

'E-e-evning, Sally,' he managed to say, before looking away quickly.

Her voice was soft, reminding him of the warm breezes of early spring. Sometimes, he wanted to curl up and go to sleep with her voice wrapped around him. There were times when he wanted to touch her black skin with the tips of his fingers as if he was stroking the high, deep night sky. But Sally wouldn't want him to do something like that. He knew that.

'Been missing you in the field, Ras.'

'Master put me to working with the white carpenter.'

'Ain't you the lucky one!' she exclaimed.

He shrugged.

'It's all the same.'

'I reckon,' she agreed.

The door of the cabin opened and a tall dark man, his face covered by a full white beard stepped out.

'Thought I heard you, Sally,' he said in a loud, strong voice.

'Evening, Uncle Isaac,' the girl smiled. 'How're you this evening?'

'Doing all right for an old man,' he chuckled, sitting down beside Ras.

'Don't say that too loud,' she responded.

'Master Lindsay will put you back out in the field.'

Uncle Isaac chuckled.

'Don't I know it! He come down here last week talking about how he could use another hand in the field. Told him I was too old to be working in that hot sun all day. Told him that he put me in the field, I might not be in any shape to haul his tobacco into town for the auction come fall,' he chuckled again. 'Well, he backed off, then. He knows that there ain't nobody in the state of Maryland who can grade and bale tobacco as good as me. He'd be lost without me. He told me to rest up and take it easy.'

Uncle Isaac laughed loudly. His laugh was one that enjoyed laughing. When others heard it, they found themselves smiling and laughing to themselves, though they didn't know what had been said. It didn't matter. Uncle Isaac laughed, and it was as if you were being tickled on the bottoms of your feet by invisible fingers.

'Uncle Isaac,' Sally began, when she had managed to stop her laughter, 'if you were younger, I'd marry you.'

The old man snorted.

'Huh! What age got to do with it? Sit down here, girl! Let an old man show you what these young ones can't.'

And he laughed even louder. Ras laughed with them. He wished he could think of funny things to say as easily as Uncle Isaac, wished that his laugh made other people happy just to hear it. But after he said 'Good evening,' he never knew what was supposed to come next.

Maybe he was afraid to tell Sally that when he saw her, he felt like a tiny bird hopping from limb to limb in a tree on an April day. But he didn't want to come in from the field one day and feel like a tree chopped down by a double-headed axe when he learned that she had been sold away. So, he said, 'Good evening,' and fell into a silence as deep and still as a well.

Scarcely a week had passed before Ras knew the names of all the tools, could saw as straight as any man Jakes had known, and put a nail through a two-by-four so quick, you had to look twice to be sure he hadn't used a sledge. If Ras had known how to read, write and do figures, Jakes could have made him into a first rate carpenter. But something gave Jakes the feeling that Ras could build the next tobacco barn without anybody's help.

Some people were like that. Learned by

doing, but couldn't read their name if it was written in letters ten feet high. Nonetheless, Jakes was enjoying teaching Ras what to do and the various ways of doing it. To Jakes' surprise, he never had to explain anything to Ras more than once, and sometimes, Ras seemed to know before Jakes finished talking.

Jakes liked to talk and though Ras never responded, Jakes talked all day, remembering all the good times he had had up in Calais, Maine (which he pronounced, Cal-lus). And on one of those afternoons, while talking about how beautiful and peaceful it was in Calais, and how he wished Ras could go there, he had an idea.

He thought about it for several days, and the more he thought the more he liked it. Now that would sure give him something to talk about when he got back. And when he got to be an old man, he could tell his grandchildren about how he had helped a pitiful, coloured boy escape from slavery. Even better would be to take Ras back when he went. That way Jakes could teach him to read and write, show him how to walk into a store and buy a suit of clothes, and how to hold his head up and look a man in the eye.

'You ever think about being free?' Jakes

asked Ras eagerly the next morning.

'No, sir,'

'What?' he exclaimed, shocked. That wasn't what he had expected Ras to say. 'What's wrong with you people? You mean to tell me that you're happy spending your life as a slave?'

'Yes, sir,' came the dull reply.

Jakes started to tell Ras just how dumb he was, but stopped, wondering suddenly if Ras was dumb. After all, what would he have said to such a question if he'd been Ras and Ras him? Would he have trusted a white man who just opened his mouth and started gabbing about being free? He knew he wouldn't.

Jakes decided that he would just talk. He was sure Ras would drink in every word like a mule drinking water after swallowing the dust of the field all day.

'Bet you didn't know that the next state north of here is a free state.'

Ras didn't respond, but took another nail from his teeth and began hammering.

'This here is Maryland,' Jakes continued, raising his voice above the sound of the hammer. 'You go north from here and in four, five days of steady walking, you're in Pennsylvania. That's a free state. Not a slave in it. Lot of free coloured people there. Some of them dress better than any white man, too.'

Jakes glanced at Ras, but couldn't tell if he was listening. But he continued, telling Ras about Philadelphia and New York and Boston.

'Too many people in those cities for me. I like a small place, like Calais. Little bitty place, right on the border between the United States and Canada. Canada is a whole separate country. Fact is, Calais is the last town in these United States. You leave Calais, walk a couple of miles and you're in another country. Done it many a day.'

Jakes talked about the winters when it snowed from October to May. It was hard to describe snow to someone who had never seen it.

'It's like rain, except it's white and cold, and stays on the ground. Sometimes the snow on the ground is taller than a man.'

Every day Jakes thought of something else to tell Ras.

'I don't know what I like better – getting up early in the morning, taking my rifle and going out to hunt deer, or going out to sit on a boulder and fishing in a fast-moving stream. And let me tell you, as far as I'm concerned, there is nothing in this world better than the sweet, soft flesh of a fish for good eating. Just thinking about it makes me want to get off this barn, and walk all the way back to Calais right now.'

When summer ended and the barn was finished, Jakes could only conclude that his words had bounced off Ras' woolly head and disappeared in the air, because not once had Jakes detected even a flicker of interest. Ras never asked any questions, never smiled, never nodded or shook his head. He just took a nail from the side of his mouth and hammered it through a piece of lumber. If Jakes had wasted his breath talking to a chicken all summer, at least the chicken would've clucked every now and then.

Well, he didn't care. Why should he? Ras didn't have any worries. He had a place to live, food to eat. Not like a white man who had to get out and earn the money to put a roof over his head and food in his belly. No. Ras wasn't dumb. Why should he want to be free like Jakes, free to starve, free to sleep in the woods, which he, Jakes, had done many a night, and would probably do again.

Ras reached his hand gingerly into the hot ashes, and jerked out the oatmeal cake. He let it lie on the floor to cool for a minute before breaking off a piece to put in his mouth. He chewed slowly, frowning as he tasted the mushy, uncooked centre. He considered returning the cornmeal cake to the embers, but was afraid that he would let it overcook this time. So he broke off another piece, and let it slide down his throat.

'Uncle Isaac?' he called, softly, through the dark interior of the cabin.

The old man lay on his plank at the other side of the room, and when Ras heard him mumble, he knew that Uncle Isaac had fallen asleep. But he had to know.

'What is it, son?' Uncle Isaac said, sleepily.

'Uncle Isaac? Have you ever eaten fish?'

'Fish?' Uncle Isaac asked, sharply, fully awake now. 'What're you asking me something like that for?'

'You ever eaten any?' Ras persisted.

Uncle Isaac rose slowly and moved over to the fireplace where he sat down on the floor next to Ras.

'When I was slaving on the Forrest Plantation in Virginia. There was a stream run right through the plantation, and master let us catch as many fish as we wanted.'

'Did?' Ras asked, amazed.

'I dream about that sometime, you know.

14

I sure do. Master Forrester let his slaves have their own garden, too.'

'Did?' Rass repeated, unable to comprehend a slave master being so kind.

'Son, me and Jessie would grow collard greens, spinach, carrots, and all like that. I hated it when Master Forrester died and his son sold me and Jessie over here. Master Lindsay is one of the stingiest masters I've ever seen.' The old man shook his head in disbelieving dismay. 'But that's not what you asked me about. What you want to know about fish for?'

Ras looked at Uncle Isaac as if he had never seen him before. Just think! He lived with someone who had actually eaten fish!

'What did it taste like, Uncle Isaac?' Ras asked, his voice brimming with reverence.

Isaac's eyes were flooded suddenly with tears.

'Don't want to talk about it,' he said, gruffly. 'Don't do no good to think about them days. It makes tomorrow harder when I think about yesterday.'

'I bet it was good,' Ras said, his eyes shining.

Uncle Isaac stood up abruptly, wiping has eyes vigorously.

'Always did make my eyes tear when I sat too close to the fire,' he mumbled. 'Believe I'll go sit out in the cool a while.'

It was late, and as Uncle Isaac sat on the porch step, he could not hear a sound from the cabins lining the quarters. There weren't even the dull yellow points of candlelight to be seen between the cracks of the cabins.

He wiped his eyes again, but that did not stop the tears or the trembling in his stomach as he remembered the look in Ras' eyes. He'd had that look once. But there'd been Jessie to think about. And life in slavery with her was better than being a free man without her. So, time passed, the look faded from his eyes, and the laugh grew. Laughing was a way of being free, too.

He supposed he'd been lucky. He and Jessie had never been sold away from each other. But the tears spilled from his eyes to trickle down his face, and behind the tears, his eyes acquired a gleam that shone with the hardness of the sun on the blade of a hoe. And he wondered, as he had so many times, if it would not have been better if they had at least tried to run away.

He knew that the three children Jessie birthed didn't die because they were sickly.

The way she cried told him the truth. Even after she was too old to birth babies, he would be awakened in the night by the sound of her crying in her sleep.

She smothered them babies with her own hands. He never saw one of them alive. Each time when the midwife called him in, the babies were dead. Looked big and healthy to him. But they didn't grow up to be slaves.

He never said anything to Jessie about it, and she never said anything to him. Sometimes, though, he would look at her while they were working in the field, and her face would be so wet with tears she looked like someone had thrown a gourd of water on her.

The night Ras came to the quarters and found his mother had been sold away, Uncle Isaac didn't ask Jessie, and she didn't say a word to him. She went to the boy, and Uncle Isaac went to find straw for him to sleep on. Jessie stopped crying in her sleep. He was glad that the last five years of her life she didn't have to cry, anymore.

Uncle Isaac wiped his face. Ras, he didn't have a Jessie to change the gleam into a laugh. He was a good boy, but the crying and laughing seemed caught inside him, like a rabbit in a trap that would never be free.

Uncle Isaac chuckled. Fish. Then he laughed aloud, and his deep voice seemed to rumble forth from some deep hole behind the stars. Fish! That was as good a reason as any for wanting to be free.

Thomas McMahon was a fat, bald, white man, who sweated profusely, summer and winter. Uncle Isaac had never seen him when he wasn't mopping his round, slick head with a big, red handkerchief and breathing noisily, as if he had just finished running five miles. Now, that would have been a sight!

Yet, of all the white men Uncle Isaac knew, Thomas McMahon was the one. It was more than a feeling Uncle Isaac had about him, though the feeling was important. But McMahon was the only white man in that part of Maryland who didn't own slaves. Uncle Isaac guessed that he still had about a hundred acres left from all he'd sold over the years. But with a hundred acres he could've been a rich man, if he owned slaves. But except for the few acres he planted in tobacco, vegetables and hay, his land was overgrown with trees and underbrush. And God was perhaps the only one who remembered the last time his house had been painted. The barn was beginning to lean as if there were a constant wind blowing against it. He was a strange man, but he was the one.

Almost absentmindedly, Isaac ran the tip of his forefinger over his thumbnail. It was as hard and thick as the blade of a plow, but it was the mind behind the nail that made the difference. It took a man who knew tobacco better than he knew himself to look at a tobacco plant and know precisely where to cut the top with his thumbnail. That was what made the tobacco grow large, sometimes seven feet high with leaves six feet long.

Uncle Isaac had heard white men offer Master Lindsay $2,000 for him. That was a lot of money for an old slave who did no heavy work. But Master Lindsay wouldn't think of selling him. Isaac was allowed to hire himself out, though, to the other planters. But he had to give half of what he earned to Master Lindsay. Uncle Isaac supposed if Jessie was still alive he would've spent the money and bought chairs, a table, clothes, and food. But caring about such things died when she died. He kept the money in a sack which he hid behind loose bricks in the fireplace.

As Uncle Isaac made his way through the

19

woods that Sunday afternoon, he didn't think what he would do if Mr McMahon turned him down. There wasn't another white he'd dare present such an idea to – not if he cared about his life. But when he remembered all the years he had used his thick thumbnail on Mr McMahon's tobacco, and how Mr McMahon always invited Isaac to sit in the shade of the porch and drink a big glass of lemonade and then talk all afternoon, Isaac knew. Thomas McMahon was the one.

When McMahon looked up from the shade of the porch where he sat in his rocking chair and saw Isaac walk out of the woods, he wondered how old Isaac was now. He looked as old and eternal as God with the big white beard like clouds around his black face. But he walked as easily as any young man, and certainly more nimbly than McMahon had ever walked. Isaac had to be eighty if he was a day. Any slave who lived that long was not only strong but wise in the ways of a wicked and hard world. And that made Thomas wonder, Why was Isaac coming to see him on a Sunday afternoon?

'Afternoon, Mr McMahon,' Isaac said, easily, as he crossed the dusty yard the chickens had picked clean of grass.

'Howdy, Isaac,' McMahon returned, in his high-pitched nasal voice that reminded Isaac of a weak train whistle.

Uncle Isaac stopped at the edge of the porch, and the two men stared at each other for a moment. Thomas mopped his head with the big red handkerchief, and looked in to the dark eyes embedded in the black face. He shifted uncomfortably, knowing it was insolent for a black to stare him in the eye like that. For an instant, McMahon wished he was the kind of white man who would've knocked Isaac down for looking anywhere else except on the ground.

'It's strange to see you over here, Isaac,' he said, coolly. 'You took care of my tobacco a while back, as I recall.'

'Yes, sir,' Isaac returned, evenly.

McMahon couldn't withstand Isaac's stare any longer, and he wiped his face with the big handkerchief to escape from those eyes.

'What can I do for you?'

'Nothing for me, sir,' Isaac smiled.

McMahon wanted to be annoyed. Why didn't Isaac just say what he wanted? But that wasn't his way. He made you come to him, and despite himself, Thomas McMahon knew he would.

'Mind if I set down here on the step, sir, and rest these old bones?'

'Sit if you want to,' Thomas returned, gruffly.

Isaac sat down, his back to the fat man in the rocking chair.

'Your tobacco turned out right well.'

'Can't complain.'

'Right well,' Isaac repeated. 'You plant about four acres, don't you, sir?'

'You know that as well as I do.'

Isaac ignored the ragged edge of annoyance in McMahon's voice. He nodded slowly, and then, turned and stared directly into the white man's eyes.

'I always thought it was strange that a man with as much land as you own wouldn't plant thirty, forty acres of tobacco.'

His voice was no longer casual, and his statement sounded like a challenge and rebuke.

'I do all right,' McMahon managed to say, startled by the abrupt change in the conversation. 'What business is it of yours?'

Isaac smiled and turned back to stare over the field where the tobacco was growing.

'It must've hurt you mighty bad when you had to sell off another twenty acres last year.'

McMahon's face turned even redder than

its normal strawberry colour.

'What's it to you?'

'When you sold that land, I thought you was going to buy you some slaves for sure this time, and plant the hundred acres you got left in tobacco, so you could earn some money to do you some good.'

'You got some slaves you want to sell, Isaac?' McMahon asked, sarcastically.

Isaac laughed.

'Now wouldn't that be something? A black man with slaves to sell.'

He laughed loudly, and just when Mc-Mahon began his tittering wheezy laugh, Isaac turned his whole body around and spoke firmly.

'I got a slave I want to free,' he said.

McMahon felt his jaw drop, and the sweat slide off his head and down his face.

'Are you crazy?' he gasped, wiping his face and neck nervously. 'I could have you whipped to within a inch of your life if I told Lindsay what you just said.'

'But you wouldn't,' Uncle Isaac said, with quiet confidence. 'Not if I know anything about people.'

'What . . . what do you mean?' Thomas McMahon asked, unable to hide his curiosity, believing in spite of himself that this old black man was about to answer for him the riddle his life had been.

'It took me a while to understand it, Mr McMahon,' Isaac said, conversationally. 'I'd think about you with almost two hundred acres of rich land, good land. And I've watched you sell off half of it over the years. And it didn't make sense, I'd say to myself, now here's a white man who could be one of the richest slaveowners in the state of Maryland, but he scarcely lives better than poor white trash. So I asked myself, why would a man who could be rich deprive himself?'

'Well, you know so much. What's the answer?' McMahon asked, with obvious, forced anger.

Isaac smiled softly.

'Because he can't bring himself to do what other men do to make themselves rich.'

'Maybe,' Thomas allowed, after a long pause. 'Maybe,' he repeated, adding hurriedly, 'But that don't mean I'm a fool! I don't know what you have schemed up, but let me tell you this. I don't plan on going to jail for helping a slave get free. And that's final!'

Isaac erupted into a big laugh.

'Jail? Who's talking about jail, Mr McMahon? I'm talking about New York.'

Thomas stared at Isaac for a moment and when he understood, a smile spread slowly across his chubby red face. He wiped his head and chuckled.

'Isaac, if you weren't so old and decrepit, I'd take a horsewhip to you for putting ideas in the head of an old, fat white man whose never done much with his life.' He laughed. 'You think it'll work?'

'I know it will, sir, I know it will.'

And the two men laughed until tears streamed down their faces, and then they laughed some more.

It was the last Sunday in September when Thomas McMahon gave a low whistle and the two horses jerked into motion, pulling the wagon filled with bales of tobacco. The sun was showing orange over the horizon as Thomas began his annual trip to New York to sell his tobacco.

In past years he had dreaded this trip, necessitated by the dislike other planters and white people had for a man who freed the slaves he had inherited from his father. If he had known then how long they would refuse to do business with him, he might have kept the slaves. Forty years had passed, but they hadn't forgotten. He still had to take his tobacco to another area in order to sell it.

He had only wanted to do the right thing as a young man of twenty-two. But what had been right for those poor blacks had been a disaster for his own life. He supposed he could have sold the plantation and moved North, but McMahons were known to be stubborn. So he'd stayed and gotten so fat he could scarcely fit into a rocking chair. It was as if he had been punishing himself for being different. Two hundred and eighty pounds of blubber sitting on the porch and watching the weeds grow. Yet, an old black man, as ancient as the Big Dipper and as a wise as the earth, who knew how to turn a tiny seed into a seven-foot-high tobacco plant, had seen something worthwhile in him.

When he got back he would ask Isaac how he had managed to see beneath all the fat, and know that Thomas McMahon hated slavery. Thomas had always believed that he'd freed his father's slaves because he was too lazy to run a plantation. But he knew now that he hadn't wanted to remember the times his father had made him watch a slave whipped. That he hadn't wanted to remember the light-skinned children he'd known were his half-brothers and sisters and whom he couldn't call that, and he hadn't wanted to remember the days his father had taken him to slave auctions to teach him how to judge what he called nigger flesh. Thomas hadn't wanted to remember, so he'd convinced himself that he was too lazy, and set the thirty slaves free.

This Sunday morning, it was thirty-one. Thomas chuckled as he thought about the tobacco tied in the wagon behind him. Even if he told someone, they wouldn't believe that at the bottom of the wagon, wrapped inside a bale of cured tobacco leaves was a young black man whom Isaac called Ras.

Ras stared through the window of his room in the white house on Center Street in Calais, Maine, marvelling yet again at the snow piled high outside. Two months had passed since the night he had unrolled himself from the tobacco leaves outside the warehouse in New York City, where Thomas McMahon took his tobacco to sell. Only two months. It seemed like a life lived by someone else.

If anyone from that life had seen him now, they would not have recognised the erect man in the dark suit with the cravat at his throat. And if they had asked his name, he would have answered proudly, Ras McMahon. His land-lady called him, Mr McMahon, and only occasionally did he forget that she was speaking to him. Once, while walking along the street, he happened to see a smiling reflection in a store window, and walked half a block before realising that it had been him. That's what freedom looked like, he concluded.

The days passed with a leisureliness that was almost mysterious. It was a curious feeling to sleep as long and as often as he wanted, to eat fish until his stomach ached. With the money Uncle Isaac had given him, Ras would not have to work until spring, at least. Calais was a lumber town and he knew he could swing an axe as good as any man. Being free now, he thought he could fell a tree with a single swing. Free! It was such a tiny word for something so big.

It was early on a cold morning, at the end of November, when the door of his room was flung open, suddenly. Ras awoke immediately, and sat up in bed to stare at a gun in the hand of Master Lindsay.

'There you are, you scoundrel!' Lindsay exclaimed.

'I told you! I told you!' came a voice from

the hallway, a voice vaguely familiar to Ras. But before he could remember where he had heard it, Jakes Brown walked hurriedly into the room.

'That's him!' Jakes said, excitedly, his eyes going nervously from the still and silent Ras to the room's pink wallpaper and back.

'I saw him walking down the street one day, dressed as fancy as a white man. Now, where's that reward money you mentioned when I wrote you?'

Lindsay reached in his coat pocket, and handed a pouch to Jakes.

'Twenty five silver pieces, like I promised.'

Jakes grinned greedily, opening the pouch and thrusting his fingers inside.

'Thanks, Ras. I might've starved to death this winter without you,' he said, laughing nervously, and hurrying from the room and out the door.

'Well, Ras. What you got to say for yourself?'

Ras' eyes widened as he looked at his master, and suddenly tears rolled down his face.

'Oh, Master! Master!' he sobbed. 'Master John! You don't know how glad I am to see you. You don't know!'

Lindsay was startled.

'What're you talking about?' he asked, warily.

'Oh, Master! Running away was the biggest fool thing this here black boy ever did. It's so cold up here, Master! And the white people up here, they don't treat a black man good like you do. Master, I'm so glad you come for me! So glad, Master!'

Ras sprang from the bed and ran across the room where he threw his arms around Master Lindsay's knees and hugged him.

'Oh, Master! I just didn't know what to do without you telling me. I didn't know when to get up and when to go to sleep.'

Master Lindsay laughed with delight.

As soon as Ras and Master Lindsay returned to the plantation, the slaveowner called all the slaves together.

'You know Ras. He ran away up North. I want you to listen to what he has to say.'

Ras stood on the porch of the big house, and looked out over the crowd of slaves gathered in the yard beneath him, and at Sally directly in front, with tears in her eyes.

Ras forced his mouth into a big grin.

'It sure is good to see you all. You don't

know how much I missed you. I didn't know how good living here was until I got up North. I didn't know how much I needed a good master like Master Lindsay to tell me what to do until I went up North. I'm so happy to be back here with Master, who'll put a roof over my head, and food in my belly and tell me what to do. And if I need anything, all I got to do is ask Master, and if he thinks I need it, then he'll give it to me.' Ras looked at his master. 'Thank you, Master. Thank you for giving this ignorant slave one more chance. Thank you, Master.'

Master Lindsay smiled.

'That's a good boy, Ras. Now, I hope you all heard him,' he declared to the slaves shivering in the chill of a cloudy autumn afternoon. 'Ras is a smart boy, and I hope you will be as smart. Now, to celebrate Ras being back, I'm giving you all the rest of the day off.'

Lindsay was surprised that his announcement was not greeted with cheers and grins. The slaves moved away quickly. Some glanced over their shoulders at Ras as if he were a dead man they wished had stayed buried.

Ras followed slowly and when he reached the slave quarters, everyone had gone into their cabins. The closed doors looked like walls to him. But as he went up the steps to the cabin he had shared with Uncle Isaac, he heard a door open. Turning, he saw Sally running across the clearing toward him.

He smiled.

'It's good to see you, Sally.'

She slapped him so hard he tasted blood in his mouth.

'Listen good, Ras!' she said, angrily. 'Listen good, because this is the last time you'll hear my voice or that of any other slave around here. I just hope you feel good after walking over a dead man's grave the way you did up there at the big house.'

'What're you talking about?' he asked, holding his cheek and swallowing a thin trickle of blood.

'Don't you know?' she exclaimed, loudly.

'Know what?'

She laughed harshly.

'Well, this is going to be a pleasure. That Monday morning, after it was clear you'd run away, Master Lindsay came down here to the quarter and asked Uncle Isaac where you were. Uncle Isaac say he don't know. Master Lindsay didn't believe him. He hung Uncle Isaac from that big oak back of the big house, tied him upside down by his ankles, and then whipped the back off him. Blood was dropping off him so fast, it sound like rain. You hear me? But everytime Master Lindsay ask him where you were, Uncle Isaac don't say a word. And when he died, he still hadn't said one word.' Tears of anger and sorrow poured down Sally's face. 'So I hope you proud of yourself. You better be, 'cos you gon' be one lonely man around here.'

She spun away, but Ras grabbed her arm and pulled her back to him. She raised her free arm to strike him, but Ras grabbed that arm and held her tightly.

'Now you listen!' he said, in a low and ominous voice. 'I'm real sorry about Uncle Isaac. Real sorry. But I ain't got no time for tears now. If you believed all you heard me say up at the big house, then you a bigger fool than Master Lindsay.'

'What?' Sally exclaimed, softly.

'What do you think he would've done to me if I hadn't said all that? He would've sent me to join Uncle Isaac in the boneyard! Don't you have any sense, woman?' he said, fiercely, flinging her away from him.

Sally looked at him unable to believe that this was Ras standing before her, his body bursting with strength. Freedom must be more wonderful that she had ever dreamed.

'Ras?' she offered, wonderingly. 'I ... I'm sorry. I should've known better.'

He nodded and Sally returned to his side to let her hand rest softly in his.

'I know about Uncle Isaac. Master told me on the trip back from the North. I didn't cry then. I'm not going to cry now.' Then, looking down into Sally's eyes, he said firmly, 'Ain't none of us gon' cry anymore, Sally.'

John Lindsay was furious when he discovered five slaves missing a month after Ras returned. Ras was furious, too, and when all the slaves had been called to the big house, he gave an even better speech than the first one.

'Them slaves what run away is just ungrateful! Master done taken care of them when they was sick, given them food, a place to live and work to do. I met white folks up North that would be happy to have what we got down here.'

The slaves nodded in agreement, and that night, laughed themselves to sleep.

Lindsay and other planters searched a week for the missing slaves. In the course of one day's futile searching, a planter mentioned that

Thomas McMahon had gone to New York to sell more of his tobacco.

'I wish he would stay there,' another planter commented bitterly, and thought no more of it.

Through the mild winter and into early spring, slaves continued disappearing, and Ras sympathised with Master Lindsay.

'They just hard-headed, Master. I feel sorry for them.'

'Speaking of being sorry,' Lindsay began, 'I been meaning to tell you something. You remember Jakes Brown, don't you?'

Ras would never forget him.

'I got a letter recently from someone I met up there in Maine, and they told me that Brown killed himself. Shot himself in the head. I feel more sorry for him than I do those dumb slaves who think they're going to be better off in the North.'

The next month, five more slaves disappeared one night. Master Lindsay was afraid now. That many slaves couldn't disappear without help from someone. The other planters agreed, and one rainy night, they met at Lindsay's to talk the matter over.

As they sat around the long oak table in the dining room after dinner, they scarcely noticed Amos pouring the snifters of brandy and passing around a box of cigars. With the death of Uncle Isaac, the grey-haired old man was the oldest slave on the plantation. He had been butler in the big house before John Lindsay was born, and was as much a part of the place now as the tobacco in the fields. That was how the planters regarded him, thinking that, like tobacco, he didn't have ears.

The slaveowners smoked cigars, sipped brandy and admitted that if someone was running slaves off the Lindsay place, it was only a matter of time before slaves started disappearing from their plantations. After more cigars and more brandy, they agreed that they had to hire armed guards to patrol their plantations every night from sundown to sun-up. It would be expensive, but losing slaves was disastrous.

'Sometimes I wonder if Tom McMahon isn't the smartest one of us all,' a planter commented.

'What do you mean?' another asked, sharply.

'Well, sometimes I wonder, who is the real slave? Us or them? We're as much enslaved to them, if not more. How many of you go to sleep at night worrying if you're going to wake up in the morning and find your barns burned down, or the legs of your mules busted.'

'You got a point there,' someone else put in.

'Sometimes I wonder if that's what Tom figured out forty years ago, and that's why he let them prime slaves go free.'

Another man chuckled.

'Well, I don't know about that, but I do know ol' Tom must have himself a lady friend up there in New York.'

'How so? Tom McMahon with a lady friend?' somebody laughed.

'I know it don't make sense, him with a lady. But seems like every month here recently, he's been going up to New York. All his tobacco was sold last fall. So what else would take him to New York if not some lady he met up there.'

'Just goes to prove what we've known all along. A Yankee woman will love anything.'

The men started to laugh, but the laughter was stopped abruptly by the sound of John Lindsay's fist hitting the table so hard that cigars perched on the edges of ashtrays fell off.

'We're a bunch of fools!' Lindsay exploded. 'A bunch of fools!'

There was a stunned silence as the realisation settled through the room that McMahon had been running off the slaves.

'Well, if it wasn't raining cats and dogs, I'd say let's go to his place and burn everything we can set fire to,' someone said, at last.

'There's always tomorrow night,' Lindsay said, with finality.

On that, the meeting ended, and the planters dispersed quickly into the stormy night.

It was late before Amos was able to sneak away from the big house and go down to the slave quarters where he told Ras what he had overheard.

'Thank you, Amos,' Ras said, when the old man finished.

'I'm not doing it for you,' the old man said, haughtily. 'I know what you been doing. Master Lindsay don't know about your part in it, yet.'

'You going to tell him?' Ras asked, menacingly.

'If it was just you, I would've told him a long time ago.'

'Then why?'

'This is for Isaac. Master Lindsay shouldn't have done that. I've known him since he was a little baby that wasn't able to turn from his back to his belly. I never thought he'd grow up to do something like he did to Isaac.'

'Thank you anyway, Amos. And if you don't hurry back to the big house, Master Lindsay might do something to you.'

Amos smiled at that.

'Oh, no. Not me. I practically raised him.'

While Amos was passing his information to Ras, John Lindsay lay awake in his big feather bed, thinking. He was thinking about Thomas McMahon's trips to New York and wondering if McMahon had made a trip around the time Ras ran away. He wondered, too, why no slaves had run away while Ras was gone, but so many had since he had returned.

He would have gone to sleep with these thoughts, if he had not heard a door closing on the ground floor of the house. He got out of bed quickly, slipping into his bathrobe. Lighting the candle on the nightstand beside his bed, he took his pistol from beneath the pillow and went rapidly and quietly down the stairs. There, in the kitchen, water dripping off him, stood Amos.

'I didn't mean to make so much noise as to wake you, Master,' Amos smiled.

'Where you been?' Lindsay asked, roughly.

Amos took off his wet coat.

'I thought I heard some noise coming from

the quarter. I thought some of them trifling slaves might be trying to make off in the rain.'

Lindsay grabbed Amos by the arm, and put the pistol to his head.

'Amos, I know you better than you think. And I know you wouldn't go out in the rain if it was Judgement Day. Now what were you doing down in the quarter? You weren't telling Ras about the meeting tonight, were you?'

The old butler was surprised that he was not afraid.

'Are you going to do me like you did Isaac?' he asked, calmly.

Lindsay released Amos, and without a word, returned to his room where he dressed warmly against the chilly rain outside. Maybe he had lost his touch. Maybe he was getting too old to handle slaves. Come spring, he would sell them all – including Amos – move to New Orleans or Savannah, Georgia, and go into business.

Shoving his pistol in his pocket, John Lindsay went out into the night.

Though there was no light as yet, Ras and Sally could see the dim outline of the foot bridge ahead.

'How far do you think we come?' Sally

whispered.

'Don't know,' Ras lied, knowing that the heavy rain had made travelling difficult. They had not come very far at all.

'Are we going to stop and rest soon?'

'As soon as we cross that bridge, we'll find a place to hide during the day and get some rest.'

'I hope it's a sunny place. I'm so wet and chilly, I'm afraid I'll catch my death.'

Ras had woken Sally minutes after Amos left, and they had started immediately. He would have preferred to have waited until the next night and gotten an earlier start. But if Master Lindsay had figured out about Mr McMahon, it wouldn't take him long to realise who had been taking the slaves to Mr McMahon.

'Let's go,' Ras whispered.

They stepped out of the woods. The stars overhead were fading before dawn as they crossed the clearing and started across the bridge. Beneath them, running through the deep gorge, they heard the thunder-roar of the river swollen by the torrential rain of the night.

They were midway across when John Lindsay stepped out of the woods on the other side, and blocked that end of the bridge.

'Oh, Ras!' Sally screamed.

'Run, Sally! Run!' Ras yelled, pushing her away as he ran toward Lindsay, his fists clenched.

Lindsay had just pulled the pistol from his coat when Ras reached him and grabbed his wrist. The two men struggled, but Ras' bare feet could not grip the rain-wet boards of the bridge, and he slipped, pulling Lindsay down on top of him.

Lindsay struck Ras in the face, and a tiny string of blood dribbled from a corner of Ras' mouth. The white man grabbed Ras' throat with one hand, and pointed the pistol at his forehead with the other. Ras grabbed the wrist of the gun hand and pushed it up. Lindsay squeezed Ras' throat tighter and tighter. Tears came to Ras' eyes, and he began to gasp for air. His grip on the wrist of the gun hand began slipping, and he could feel Lindsay's arm coming lower and lower. The breath in his body became thinner and thinner, and though he knew the sun was rising, everything was becoming black.

Suddenly, there was the sound of a gunshot. The hand at Ras' throat relaxed, and John Lindsay fell on top of him.

'Ras! Ras! Ras!'

Ras opened his eyes slowly, grasping for air. Through his tears, he saw Sally standing above him. Master Lindsay's pistol dangling from her hand.

'Ras! You all right?'

He managed to nod. He pushed Lindsay's body off him, and got up slowly. Sally dropped the pistol, and flung herself into his arms.

'I was so afraid, Ras,' she sobbed. 'I saw him pointing that gun at your head, and I didn't know what to do, Ras. I didn't know what to do.'

Ras managed a wheezy chuckle.

'It doesn't seem that way to me,' he said.

She shook her head.

'I guess I snatched the gun out of his hand. I don't know. I just couldn't let him kill you. I just couldn't let him kill you.'

The rays of a soft and clear dawn were warming them now. Ras lifted the body of his dead master, and dropped it over the bridge, watching as it fell slowly through space and into the river so far below.

They stared into the river for a long while, watching it swirl and crash down the gorge. Sally rested her head against Ras' chest. Her body trembled with cold and fear, and he pressed her to him.

43

'Let's go,' he said, finally. 'We need to sleep.'

'Not yet, Ras,' she said, quietly. 'Not just yet. I-I feel so strange.'

He looked at her, and was surprised to see a smile on her lips. He knew that smile and the tremulous flutterings in the stomach that went with this strange, new feeling of freedom.

'Let's go,' he repeated, quietly, hugging her even tighter. You'll have the rest of your life to get used to that feeling.'

She shook her head.

'It's too good to get used to, Ras. I want being free to feel like this always.'

And so did he. So did he.

Author's note

'This strange, new feeling' is a true story based on an account published in *The Anglo African Magazine*, Vol. 1, No. 10, October 1859, pp. 321–4. The characters of Ras, Jakes Brown and the slave owner are taken from that account.

Where the sun lives

When the overseer rings the bell to wake the field hands, it is not daybreak yet. Sometimes, if Mistress Phillips has had a bad night, I am awake and hear the bell. I am jealous of the field hands, because they have slept through the night. Their work has a beginning and an end. Sometimes, mine has pauses.

Last night Mistress Phillips' fever came back. I sleep on the floor at the foot of her bed. When I was a little girl, I slept lying across her feet to keep them warm, a thin blanket over me. She used to turn from her back to her stomach to her side throughout the night, and I would get kicked.

I'm bigger and older now. Mammy Sukey said she thinks I'm eighteen. In the winter I sleep in the bed with Mistress Phillips to help her stay warm. Before Master moved to the other bedroom, I slept in the bed with both of them. In the summer I sleep on the floor. Sometimes, I wonder what it would be like to sleep without being waked, to sleep through the night and through the day and through the night again.

Mistress Phillips coughs, and I hold the basin under her chin as she retches. She sinks back into the bed, hatred in her eyes as she stares at me. That don't mean nothing. She hates me because she's dying, and I'm not. I guess she's angry, because she's always had me to do whatever she wanted. Now, she wants me to die for her and I can't.

'Master be here with the doctor soon,' I tell her.

She just stares at me. She know the doctor can't do no good. He might take a little blood, but that don't seem to help. I guess don't nothing help when you dying – except to die and be done with it.

I get up from the side of the bed.

'Where you going, Maria?' comes her hoarse voice.

'Just to raise the window, Mistress. Let some of the cool morning air in for you.'

I cross the room and raise the shade of the window that looks out over the yard and down to the slave quarters. I see a man on a horse, a black man riding slow and quiet, like he doesn't want to wake the morning too rudely. He rides up through the slave quarter, and past the stand of pine trees. There's a big heavy-looking sack tied across the horn of his saddle. I can't see his face in the light of false dawn, but he must be handsome. I know, because you can tell a lot about a person from the way they walk or the way they sit on a horse. He sits on that horse like it is part of him. He's past the overseer's shack, and is headed toward the stable. If I didn't know better, I would swear he knew where the sun lives.

'Maria!'

'Yes'm,' I respond, raising the window quickly and hurrying back to the bed. 'I'm right here.'

'What were you looking at out that window?

'Nothing. Just looking. That's all.'

'When I get well, I'll give you twenty lashes for staring out that window when you're supposed to be looking after me.'

'Yes'm,' I mumble.

That's one beating I won't have to worry about. Everybody know she ain't going to lay that rawhide whip on nobody ever again. She know it, too. It's just hard for her to believe it.

She closes her eyes and I hear the rooster begin crowing down in the chicken house. I wait. Way off in the distance, over on the Bradley plantation, a rooster crows. It's like that every morning. This rooster over here crows. Then, a minute later, the Bradley rooster crows. They'll be crowing at each other for the next hour now. I wonder what they be saying to each other? Wonder if this rooster telling the Bradley's rooster about Mistress Phillips? Or maybe this rooster is telling about the black man on the horse.

I place my hand on Mistress' forehead. She knocks it away.

'I'm not dead yet,' she growls, pushing at me weakly. 'You think I'm going to die, don't you? That would make you happy, wouldn't it?'

'No'm, Mistress. No'm, it wouldn't.'

Her eyes have a wild, crazy sparkle in them as she stares at me. I stare back, trying to put as much life in my eyes as I can. I want her to see all the life that's in me, all the life that she won't be able to take from me.

She closes her eyes.

'You not going to die, Mistress.'

She knows I'm lying, but I don't think it's a sin to lie to a dying woman. Especially one whose life wasn't nothing but one long day of suffering. Mammy Sukey said Mistress was one of the prettiest girls in Virginia. Mammy remember when she was born right here in this room, in this very bed.

I remember the first time I was brought up from the quarters to be her gal. I looked at her yellow hair and it made me think of buttercups and sitting by Miller's Creek with my dusty feet in the water. I was seven then. Mistress treated me like I was her little girl. She played little games with me, and at night, would tell me stories. After she lost her first baby in the fifth month, she told me that it was all right, that I was her baby.

It was after she lost the third baby that she whipped me for the first time. I was in the kitchen that morning putting her breakfast on the big, round silver tray to bring upstairs. I turned around and she was standing in the doorway, the whip in her hand.

She told me to come outside. Then she told me to take my dress off. I was shamed to stand there in the yard as naked as when I come in the world. Mammy Sukey was pleading with Mistress, begging her to say what I had done wrong, and Mammy said she would be sure I wouldn't do it again.

Mistress Phillips say that I hadn't done nothing wrong. Just that it was time I learned that I was a slave. I ain't never felt nothing in my life as bad as the first time the whip cut my flesh. It was like somebody had taken a stick out of the fire and held it to me. I fell down in the dust, and I don't remember nothing else. Mammy Sukey say that Master Byron had to come out of the house and jerk the whip out of her hand.

Next thing I remember was waking up and I was lying in Mistress' bed. She was putting cool salve on my back and my chest, and tears were streaming out of her eyes. Mistress was saying how sorry she was and asking me to forgive her.

Soon as I was well, she didn't act like she was sorry anymore. After a while, I could tell when she was going to get the whip. It was something about the way she would wake up in the morning, a look in her face like her eyes died during the night. I don't know which I hated more – the whippings, or her taking care of me afterward.

Now, sitting here on the side of the bed watching her die, none of that seems to matter much. All that pretty buttercup-colour hair is grey now. Her skin used to be as smooth as peach fuzz and her cheeks were as red as fresh-picked-raspberries. Now, she looks like an old lady and her face is the colour of old sour milk. Mammy Sukey said Mistress Phillips will be thirty in August. That's one birthday she'll have in the boneyard.

I hear the carriage coming up the road.

'Master and the doctor coming, Mistress,' I say.

Her eyelids flutter, but do not open. She probably doesn't care. Mammy Sukey said that Mistress never did want Master to be a lawyer and go into politics. She wanted him to stay on the plantation and run everything. She had been running the plantation since she was a girl of sixteen and her momma and poppa died when their carriage overturned near Cousin's Bluff. When Mistress married Master, she thought he would run everything then, and she could be a lady and give big parties. Least, that's what Mammy Sukey say.

The carriage stops in front of the house, and in a minute I hear the front door open and the sound of boots hurrying across the floor and up the stairs.

When Master walks in, he smiles at me. Doctor Carson don't look at me, but goes straight to the bed. Master comes around to my side of the bed, and puts his hand lightly on my shoulder. I look up into his face. His black, curly hair needs a comb through it, and his eyes are red from driving all the way to Richmond and back. But he looks so young and she looks so old. I wonder if that's because he could never take the whip to any of the slaves. Mammy say that's why he decided to go into politics. He just didn't have the stomach for doing us like Mistress did.

I remember the argument they had just last month, right before Mistress took to bed for the last time. It was the day Mistress went down to the stable to get Baby, her favourite horse. I was standing behind her, just inside the stable door. Mammy Sukey's boy, Jim, takes care of all the horses, keeps them combed and pretty looking, makes sure they get just the right amount of oats and exercises them every day. With six horses to take care of, plus the mules from the field, Jim don't get much more sleep than I do.

When Mistress walked in the barn, Jim wasn't there. She called him, but he didn't come. I got scared. I don't know how I knew, but Jim had gone back to the quarters to take a nap. Mistress told me to go to the quarters to see if he was there.

He was asleep. When I woke him and he saw me, he knew he was in trouble. There's some things us slaves don't have to say out loud. We just know a lot of times what the right thing to do is.

I went back and told Mistress that he wasn't there. She said I was lying. I told her to see for herself. She went and Jim wasn't there.

That night Master and Mistress had the worse argument I ever heard. He accused her of making all the best slaves run off, told her that Jim was the best man in all Virginia when it came to caring for horses, that he was irreplaceable. She told Master that he didn't have no say in running the plantation, that he spent most of his time in Richmond drinking brandy and smoking cigars, and she would do as she pleased with her slaves.

Wasn't nothing Master could say to that, or so I thought. He don't own none of us. We wish he did. All the slaves are hers, but he told her that if he ever heard of her making another slave run off, and if she ever laid the whip on me again, he would kill her.

I heard that with my own ears. Mammy heard it and she was way out back in the kitchen. They were yelling so loud I wouldn't be surprised if folks in Richmond didn't hear. I know our old rooster had plenty to tell that morning.

When Master told Mistress he would kill her, she just fainted dead away. Me and Master carried her up to her bed, and she hasn't set foot on the floor since. Maybe she going to die just to make Master feel bad. But as I leave the room to see if Mammy has breakfast ready yet for Master and the doctor, I think Master will probably look even younger once Mistress is in the ground.

When I walk out the back door, the sun is up. The roosters always stop crowing once the sun is all the way out. It's almost like they think their crowing is what makes the sun rise, and once it's up, then it can get across the sky on its own.

I cross the few feet from the house to the building behind, which is the kitchen. I notice the thin trail of smoke rising through the chimney, which means Mammy has the fire going and is probably kneading the dough to make biscuits.

When I enter the kitchen, a man is sitting at the table drinking a glass of water. It is him. I can tell by the easy way he sits in the chair, his legs stretched out like snakes sunning on a rock down by the creek. His skin is brown and smooth like acorns. His face is serious. I could not make him smile.

He sees me, and I feel ashamed in my thin dress that is so short he can see my knees. I don't want him to see me with hair sticking out all over my head like porcupine quills. But I walk past the table, looking as if he's not even there. I lift my chin up a little, like I wouldn't stoop to speak to him if he was the last man in the world. I don't know why I act just the opposite of how I feel.

'How is she?' Mammy asks, her long thin fingers digging into the mound of dough and squeezing it quickly.

'About the same,' I say, going over to the bucket in the corner and taking a sip of water from the gourd dipper.

'Was you up again last night?'

'Yes'm. Mistress' fever was pretty bad.'

Mammy Sukey is as thin as a limb that broke off a tree in a storm. Master say she's as old as the wind. She not too much bigger than a spring breeze, but she work as hard any anybody around here. Wouldn't nothing be the same without Mammy.

She has put the kettle of water on the stove, knowing I like a good strong cup of coffee in the morning. I take a can off the shelf beside the stove and dump some coffee grounds in the water. I want to ask her about Jim, but don't dare with that man sitting there looking like he know how come cows eat green grass and give white milk. But I can tell by the calm way Mammy is rolling out the dough that Jim is still safe. Mammy will send word for him to come back when she's ready. Master won't let Mistress put the whip to Jim. Everybody knows that. About the only whipping there's going to be around here now is the one Death is putting on Mistress.

'What the doctor say?' Mammy asks as she cuts out the biscuits.

'Nothing while I was there.'

I want to turn and see if the man is staring at me like I want him to. But I keep my eyes on Mammy's bony black hands cutting circles from the white dough. I don't want to know how I would feel if he wasn't looking at me.

'Doc Carson is a good doctor, but even he can't beat ol' Death.'

His voice is soft. It makes me think of horses grazing in a meadow in the springtime.

'I suppose not,' I manage to say, turning slowly to look at him.

He is looking at me and I'm shamed, because I want him to and I don't want him to. He is looking at me, and I know he can see through my thin dress and is looking at all the ugly scars and welts on my stomach and across my breasts. Mammy Sukey said that even if I did have babies one day, I wouldn't be able to suckle them, not with breasts scarred and torn and flattened like mine.

'I'm Forrest Yates, the blacksmith,' he smiles.

'How do you do?' I say, remembering my manners. 'They call me Maria.'

'That's a pretty name.'

'Thank you.'

I'm smiling now, smiling too much, because what I really want to do is laugh. That's what I want to do.

He stands up to go.

'Thanks for the water, Mammy.'

'You don't need to be thanking me, Forrest. I don't know what I can ever do to thank you. You be careful, and don't let Jim do nothing that would jeopardize you. You hear me?'

'You needn't worry. Jim wouldn't do anything like that.'

'You come back in a hour or so, and I'll have a nice big breakfast for you. With her being sick and Master being in Richmond most of the time, I can cook up some of this good food for us.'

She laughs.

'Thank you,' Forrest says, but he is looking at me.

'That is one nice young man,' Mammy Sukey says after Mr Yates leaves.

'Yes,' I say, trying not to sound interested, but hoping she keeps talking.

'He free.'

'Free!' I exclaim.

I understand now why he rides his horse slow, like he don't have nothing else to do.

'Born free. Never slaved a day in his life. But he cares more about us slaves than a lot of us do for ourselves. White folks think the world of him, too. He's supposed to be the best blacksmith in Virginia. I heard Master say once that he wish he could find him a bootmaker to put shoes on his feet as good as the ones Forrest makes for horses.'

'How did a black man get to be born free?' I want to know.

'His mama was Mistress Bradley's serving girl, and when Mistress Bradley died, she leave it in her will that his mama was to be set free. She was carrying Forrest at the time. He missed being born a slave by three months.'

The water in the kettle is boiling now and I look at it, but it is only beginning to turn muddy. I like my coffee black.

'Hadn't you better get on back to the house to see if you needed? The coffee be here when you get back. You tell Master and the doctor that breakfast be ready in about twenty minutes, soon as these biscuits get done.'

Forrest. That's perhaps the prettiest name I've ever heard in all my life.

'Did you hear me, girl?'

'Yes'm,' I say quickly, hurrying from the kitchen.

Once outside, I stop and look toward the front of the house and across the road. The pines and oak trees and elm are silent and still in the early morning light. They are a forest, and it is cool in the forest. The birds sing and tiny animals run quickly on tiny feet across a floor of fallen leaves and pine needles. I can't help it. I laugh and laugh and laugh.

Mammy Sukey says that you can tell how evil a person was by how long it takes them to die. Mistress must've been the Devil. She was all of three months dying, and if she had lasted five more days, she would've seen her thirtieth birthday.

But last evening after supper, we heard the screech owl. That's always a sign of death.

Yesterday morning a bird flew in the house. So, we knew the end was near.

It was way up in the night when I was awakened by the sound of her thrashing in the bed. That wasn't anything new. The last month she thrashed around a lot, like she thought she could fight ol' Death off. She would thrash and curse. Cursed just about everybody in the state of Virginia, but especially her momma and poppa for getting themselves killed and leaving her alone to run a big plantation when she should've been putting on pretty dresses and going to balls in Richmond with handsome boys.

I listened to her cursing her momma and poppa for leaving her like they did, as if they wanted to or could help it. My momma and poppa left me, but I don't curse them. Maybe Mistress sold them because she wanted me to feel all alone like she did.

Last night she got to thrashing and cursing again, and then, all of a sudden, she started retching and coughing and then breathing real heavy. It sounded like there were rocks and sand in her chest. She raised up in the bed and her white hair looked like a dustrag with the moon shining on her. I was standing at the foot of the bed looking at her. She reached

out her arms for me, but I didn't move. I knew
Death had come in the room to stay this time.
I didn't want her touching me as Death put
his arms around her. Her eyes got big and they
seemed to be calling my name. I didn't move.
I just looked at her, and then she fell back in
the bed. I lay back down on the floor and
listened to her breathing. It sounded like a big
dog scratching at a door.

I didn't hear the quiet when it started. All
of a sudden I noticed, and it was like the whole
world was still. I listened to the silence and
wanted it to last forever. It felt like somebody
was touching me all over with hands as soft as
dandelion fluff. I didn't want to fall asleep, but
I must have, because the first thing I know I
am hearing the overseer ringing the bell. I
get up and stand at the window until I see
Forrest riding up through the slave quarter. I
go out to the kitchen and tell Mammy.

'When did she die?' Mammy says, sorrowfully.

'Just now.'

'Poor thing.'

I don't say anything, but go and tell the
overseer. He stands a minute looking like
Mistress' dying is an insult to him. He squirts
tobacco juice on my feet and walks off to the

slave quarters. It wouldn't be proper to have the slaves work in the fields until after her funeral. Overseer walk like he don't know what to do today with no slaves to whip.

When I get back to the house, Mammy has awakened Master. I bring him his breakfast in bed. There is no sadness in him. He sends me back to the kitchen for another helping of bacon and more biscuits. He says he wants to bury her that afternoon if Charles, the slave carpenter, can get a box made that soon. I tell him that folks might talk if he puts her in the ground so quick. He wants to know what folks, she didn't have no kin and no friends. Won't be nobody to the funeral except Master and us slaves. The overseer be the only one to shed a tear, because he won't have a job soon. Least, I hope not.

After I carry Master's dirty dishes back to the kitchen, Mammy and I go up to Mistress' room to wash her body and put her in her laying-out clothes. Her body is so smooth. There are no marks on it, not even any warts or pimples or birthmarks. Her breasts are round and big, and I don't know why, but I start crying and can't stop. Mammy puts her arms around me, thinking I'm sorrowing because Mistress is dead. But that's not it.

I run down to the stables and when Forrest sees me, he puts down the bellows he's using on the fire and holds me close to him. I cry and cry, and feeling his big, strong hands on my back shames me so much. I break out of his arms, and run and run until I cross the road and am in the forest. I lie down beneath a pine tree and cry and cry, and up in the tree I hear a squirrel squawking at me.

Mistress is lying in the box that Charles made. She is laying in the front parlour, and there are big white candles at the head and foot of the box. Master stands at the head of the box in a black suit.

I stand in the doorway between the parlour and the dining room. The last of the slaves file past to pay their respects. They pass me on one side going in, and on the other coming out. They look serious and sad as they file in, stop to look at Mistress, then shake Master's hand and say a few words to him. I'm the only one who sees the smiles on their faces as they go out.

Forrest comes in, Jim following. Master sees them, and he rushes forward to shake Jim's hand and to welcome him back to the planta-tion. You would think that Jim was his very own son. He's not. Master ain't like some slave masters who got a lot of back door children. He just likes Jim, 'cos Jim loves horses much as he do. He like Jim the way he like me. If Master like you, don't make no difference your colour.

I wonder if Master knew that Jim was hiding at Forrest's house. Probably. Some other white man would've had Forrest arrested for hiding a runaway slave. Not Master. He know. He understand how it is.

The house is empty now. Master sits in a chair at the head of the box. It wouldn't be right for him to go up to bed and leave his dead wife all alone in the night. I don't think it's right for him to have to keep the death watch all by himself, though, so I walk quietly across the polished floor and sit down by his chair.

He tells me that I can go to bed, but I say that's all right. I'd just as soon stay there with him. He don't say nothing for a long time. Maybe he's remembering, like I am, remembering the times he used to come to the house to court Mistress. I remember the second time he came and brought flowers to her and a paper sack of candy for me. He used to give me little notes to give her after he was gone.

We've known each other a long time, me

and Master. He don't know much about me, I guess, but there ain't much to know about a little slave girl. Except I ain't little now.

I know a lot about him, and I think he appreciates that I haven't ever told what I know. I didn't even tell Mammy when Master and Mistress stopped sleeping in the same bed, and that's been more than three Christmases ago. Even before that, I never told what they talked about in the night. We've known each other a long time, me and Master.

'Was there something I could've done different?' he asks me.

'No, Master. Not unless you could've brung her momma and poppa back to life. I think that's the only thing that would've made her different.'

'And she made both of us suffer for it.'

'She the one what suffer. We just hurt from time to time.'

He don't say nothing for another long while. When he does, he says what I was afraid he would say.

'How would you like to come to Richmond and cook and wash for me? There won't be nothing for you to do around here anymore.'

I look up at him. He has that shy man's look in his eyes, the way a man looks when the question he's asking is not the one he spoke. We've known each other for a long time, me and Master, and he ain't like a lot of masters are with the slave women. It ain't because he might not want to be. He just don't know how to do it and make it seem all right.

'That ain't a good idea, Master,' I say.

'You're right, Maria,' he says quickly, almost like he's glad I said what I did. 'But what're you going to do now? I've been thinking about selling all the slaves and the house, too. I'm not the man to run a plantation. And if I leave the overseer in charge, I'm afraid he'll whip everybody half to death in a year's time.'

'Yes, sir. But David Allman know as much about running this place as Mistress did. In fact, whenever she had a decision to make, she didn't talk to the ol' overseer, she talk to David. He could run the plantation for you, and me and Mammy could help him.'

He chuckles. 'You and Mammy figure this one out together?'

'No, sir. It's my idea.'

He laughs at that.

'Maria, if you weren't a slave, there's no telling what you could've been.'

'Yes, sir.'

It has been a month since Mistress died. Before Master went back to Richmond, he told me that I could sleep in Mistress' bed, and that I didn't need to do any work, except to see that everything was kept dusted and cleaned. I thanked him, but I moved into an empty cabin in the slave quarter. Mammy tried to shame me by saying I was scared to sleep in a dead woman's bed, but it's not that. I guess I'm just afraid that if I sleep in a soft bed too long, I won't know how to sleep on the floor when I get moved back there.

There is not much work. I dust and sweep and help Mammy in the kitchen. Master told her that it was all right for her to cook lunch to carry to the slaves in the field. Ol' overseer got mad about that, say Master's slaves eat better than white folks. I told him they ought to since they work harder. He turned so red I thought the blood was going to pop out of his face.

Mainly I wait for the evening. Forrest rides in about sundown. Sometimes I wait by the road, and he'll ride up, reach down and lift me on his horse. I'll wrap my arms around his waist, and we'll ride to the top of the hill and watch the sunset.

Since that first morning when I walked into

the kitchen and saw him sitting here, I don't suppose there's been a day when he hasn't come. I thought he was coming to tell Mammy how Jim was doing. She said I must be thick in the head not to know why he kept coming around.

That wasn't it. I know why I want him to come, but I don't know why he wants to come. He don't ever say, and I don't ever ask. He comes and sometimes we sit in the kitchen and talk and drink coffee, or take a walk down by the creek. He tells me about all the different plantations he works on, and all about the houses of the rich white people in Richmond and how he keeps their horses shoed and the wheels on their carriages repaired. I don't have much to say. I ain't never been anywhere and don't know nothing except what happens on this plantation. He don't seem to mind, though.

He's the most different man I've ever seen. He reminds me of Master. Forrest don't seem to be afraid of anything in the world. That must come from being born free. He can read and write, and he took a little twig once and wrote my name in the dirt. He spelled out the letters to me, pointing to each one, and that was the most wonderful thing. I didn't see how them little straight up and down marks could be me, but it was wonderful anyway. He say that one day he'll teach me to read and write any word in the world. I shook my head and said that was more than I wanted. I didn't tell him that all I wanted was to learn to read and write his name. Then I'd go all over the world and write it on everything I passed. That would be a silly thing to do, but it feels nice to think about.

Master is back from Richmond. All us slaves are worried. We think he has made up his mind to sell us and get out of the slave-owning business. For three days now, he has had me packing up all of Mistress' clothes and putting them in boxes, packing up the fine china and silverware. He's had some of the men slaves taking the best furniture to his new house in Richmond. All the while, he look serious and don't talk except to give an order. Mammy said she tried to ask him what was going on, but he just told her that she would find out when the time came. We all know what that means.

The slaves what been taking the furniture to Richmond say that Master got a big, fine house there. They believe he must be going to marry again, 'cos wouldn't no single man need a house big as that. If that's true, then I'm not worried. I know Master wouldn't sell me or Mammy or Jim.

I've finished packing all of Mistress' belongings and I go to Master's study to tell him.

'I suppose you want me to put all them boxes in the barn tomorrow,' I say, standing in the doorway and looking at him sitting behind his big desk.

'I don't reckon you'll be here tomorrow,' he say, calm like.

'Sir?' I say, feeling a large wound opening inside me.

I blink my eyes rapidly, trying not to let him see me cry.

'I sold you today,' he say, smiling.

I don't understand how he can say something like that and smile. I suppose his new wife-to-be told him to get rid of me and don't show no feeling about it.

'Yes, Master,' I mumble.

I notice my hands playing with the hem of my dress, like I'm some little baby.

'Your new master is waiting out back for you. I'm sure you'll be happy, Maria.'

'Yes, sir.'

I stand there, waiting for him to say something else. I don't know what. Maybe that he's sorry or that he appreciated all I've done. But he lowers his head and goes to reading some papers on his desk.

'That's all,' he say, looking up. But he's smiling. 'Your new master is waiting for you.'

'Yes, sir.'

I walk out of the study slowly, and for an instant, think about running out the front door, across the road and into the forest. But I don't. I walk through the parlour, the dining room, and out the back door.

I don't see anybody except Forrest, and I rush into his arms, sobbing. I don't want to tell him that I'll never see him again, but finally he quiets me, and I tell him that I've been sold.

'Where's your new master?' he asks.

'Master said he was waiting for me out here.' I look around but don't see anyone. 'I don't see nobody.'

'You don't?' Forrest asks.

I shake my head.

'I suppose I'm nobody,' he teases me.

'Oh, you know what I mean,' wondering how he can make a joke at a time like this. 'Maybe Master meant to say that he was waiting in the front of the house.'

We go to look, but there is no one there.

'Now, what exactly did your master say?' Forrest wants to know.

'He said I'd been sold, and that my new master was waiting for me in the back.'

Forrest takes my hand, and we go around the house again. No one is there.

'I don't understand it,' I say.

'Well, your master wouldn't lie to you.'

He is smiling at me, and I'm about to lose my temper and ask him how come he think my being sold is so funny, when he starts to chuckle.

'You got to call *me* master now,' he say.

I can't believe it.

'Forrest,' I say, softly.

He has a grin on his face that's so big I'm afraid he's going to break his jaw.

'Forrest!' I shriek, loud enough to wake the dead and all the angels in heaven. 'Forrest!'

Laughing, he picks me up and whirls me around and around and I'm laughing and crying and shrieking all at the same time. I still can't believe it, and when he puts me down, I demand that he tell me everything.

'Well, I went to him right after the funeral, and asked him would he set you free because I wanted to marry you. He said he couldn't do that, because it was against the law. If he set

72

you free, you would have to leave the state of Virginia. But, he said there wasn't any law against a free black man from owning a slave. Fact is, I know several who own their wife and children. By the law, they can't marry. But ain't no law say that can't live together as a family. They slaves on paper, and that paper don't mean anything. He said he had to go to Richmond for a while, and when he came back, he'd sell you to me. So, pack your things, because you coming home with me tonight.'

'Mammy! Mammy!' I scream, and run into the house, almost knocking Master down. 'Oh! I'm sorry, Master. I didn't see you standing here in the doorway.' Then I throw my arms around his neck and hug him so tight I get scared I might break his neck. 'Thank you, Master! Thank you!'

He doesn't hug me back, and when I let him go, he is smiling. It's not his real smile, but more like the one he would give Mistress whenever there was company around.

'I'm going to miss you,' he says.

'Yes, sir,' is all I can say, and he knows that I won't miss him.

Forrest rises early. Sometimes he has to ride a ways to the plantation where he'll be working that day. He tells me to go back to sleep, that he's used to getting up and fixing his own breakfast and packing a dinner. Even after two years he tells me that. I tell him what I've been telling him for two years. He can get used to letting me do it.

So, we do it together. He starts the coffee boiling on the cookstove, while I start frying up some pork chops and put the potatoes in the hot ashes in the fire place. He goes out to the barn to give the horse he's going to ride that day some fresh oats and to brush him. I watch him through the window, and every morning, it's like that first time when I saw him riding up through the slave quarters, riding slow and easy like he was brother to the sun. I sweep out the cabin and make the bed while he's down in the barn. By then, the coffee is ready, and I pour two cups and take them down to the barn. We sit on the railings of the corral and watch the sun come up.

Our house is at the top of a small hill, and I can almost see the plantation where I lived. Sometimes, I see smoke rising from behind the stand of pine trees that blocks the big house from my view, and when I do, I know that Master and his new wife are back from Richmond and Mammy is cooking up breakfast.

Forrest asked me once if I missed the plantation. I asked him if he had lost his mind. It don't make no difference how good a master is, you still a slave. Time I said it, however, I knew I should've kept my mouth shut.

That's the one thing me and Forrest argue about sometime. He say if he set me free, we would have to leave Virginia. I tell him to let's go. He say that he don't want to, that he got plenty of work around here. I tell him that a blacksmith can get work up North. He say he don't know nobody in the North and he was born and raised in Virginia and for me not to worry. He say that he has already made out his will and in there it says that I'm to be free when he dies. He say that is how his mother got free. He ask me if I trust my old master. I tell him that I do. He say that Master has the will, and Master knows I'm to go free. I tell him I understand, but I'd rest easier in my mind if I wasn't a slave on paper.

I don't want to think about that this morning. Forrest is going into Richmond today, and he say I can come to go shopping if I want. He's going to see a man who has a pretty horse for sale. We got three horses now. I don't see why we need another one, but Forrest loves horses. He says he want a fine new horse just

75

to pull the new carriage he wants to buy for me. I tell him the wagon is good enough for me. He say I don't understand.

Forrest leaves me off at the dry goods store while he goes to buy the horse. Now that I'm here, I wonder why I came. I look at all the people walking up and down the street and wonder where they came from and where they're going. It is hot and the dust hangs in the air like laundry put out to dry. I go in and out of stores, but don't buy anything. I could make better dresses when I was eight years old.

I am walking down the street when I see a large crowd. I go toward it, hoping it's the puppet show I happened on the last time I came to town. I look around eagerly at the crowd, thinking that I might see Mammy, Jim or somebody from the plantation. I don't see any black people, however.

Suddenly the crowd starts applauding and hollering. I look toward the front. There on a stage is a long, tall white man. Standing next to him is a black girl who looks no older than I was when Forrest came and took me. Her head is bowed.

'Ladies and gentlemen!' shouts the thin white man, in a shrill voice. 'Now this here is one of the finest girls you'll see in the state of Virginia. She has worked in the fields, but with the proper training, can work in the house. Obedient, docile and there's not a mark on her body.' He looks at the girl and says, 'Take it off!'

She looks at him, her eyes growing big.

'Don't be bashful now,' he says, laughing.

The crowd laughs.

'Just pull it over your head like you do for all the young bucks.'

The crowd laughs louder.

The girl crosses her arms over her breasts, and moves away from the white man. He grabs her by the arm, and snatches the top of her dress, pulling on it hard. It rips and falls to the floor. The crowd cheers loudly.

The girl doesn't know what part of her body to hide from all the eyes. The crowd laughs even more. The white man slaps at her arms, and she lets them hang limply at her side.

'Gentlemen! Now I ask you! Have you seen a finer bit of flesh on the market in the past year? I guarantee that you haven't. This girl here is good for anything you might have in mind.'

That causes more cheering and clapping.

The man tells the girl to turn around and

when she does, he grasps her buttocks and squeezes them. He turns her to face the crowd again and puts his hand on her full breasts and squeezes.

'Just as ripe as a cantaloupe off the vine with the dew still on it. Now, who'll make the first bid?'

'Five hundred!' someone in the front yells.

The girl is looking straight at the crowd now, the tears running down her face. I cannot tell for sure, but I think she is looking at me.

'Five fifty!' comes another shout.

Maybe if she looks at me, she won't cry. She'll know that we can't ever let them see us cry. If they see us cry, then we won't have anything left that's ours.

'Seven hundred!'

I guess she can't see me, because her shoulders heave as her tears become sobs. I walk away before I go up on that stage and slap her.

Forrest and I have our worse argument yet as we drive home, the shiny black horse tied to the back of the wagon. He's angry that I didn't have better sense, as he puts it, than to stay by the slave market. I tell him that I got plenty sense, better sense than him 'cos I don't want more horses than I need.

'You just can't get rid of the slave mentality is what's wrong with you,' he tells me.

I don't say anything, because if we keep talking, one of us is going to say something that we can't take back – ever. That's what made it so bad for Master and Mistress. They said things to each other that 'I'm sorry' wouldn't make go away. They said things that the other one couldn't forget, and not being able to forget it, there was nothing to do but remember.

'I shouldn't have said that,' Forrest says, after a while.

'You right,' I tell him.

'I'm sorry.'

His voice is soft and sweet like a quiet rain in the middle of the night in the springtime. I want to stay angry a while longer, but when he talks in that voice, well, something happens to me. But before I get all the way soft, I have to know.

'What you mean by saying I got a slave mentality?'

I can tell that he doesn't want to answer when he says, 'Aw, nothing. I just got hot under the collar. You had me scared.'

'If you hadn't meant something, you wouldn't have said it. I ain't never known you to waste no words, Forrest Yates.'

He sighs like he knows he's caught.

'Let me put it this way. I want us to live as good as white people. That means we got to have the things that white people do. That'll prove that we're just as good as they are.'

'And that's how come you bought a horse we don't need and are going to buy a carriage we don't need?'

'It'll prove that I'm as free as they are.'

I want to tell him that it proves that he's a bigger fool than they are, but I don't. When you love somebody, you can think they're a fool some time, but if you say it, you're the fool.

'Maybe having the slave mentality ain't all bad,' I say, finally.

'I didn't mean that, Maria,' he apologises.

'It's all right. The slave mentality sees white folk and their fine horses and big houses and pretty china and all like that. But we see that they ain't got no love. And that's all I got to say on it.'

It is a few weeks before all our wounds heal. Forrest needs to see me look at him with my eyes all soft and warm, like he is the best man in the world. I need him to look at me, his eyes all glazed over. When he looks at me like that, the scars on my body disappear and my breasts stand round and firm.

So when he rides in one evening in a carriage, I exclaim and carry on like it's the prettiest thing I've ever seen in my life. He is proud of it, and maybe he's right. Maybe a black man needs carriages and fine horses to feel that he's really free. Maybe he can't believe he's free unless he can see it. All I know is that I hope he didn't have to borrow too much money to pay for it.

But I don't say that. Instead I cook him a special dinner of chicken smothered with dumples. Afterwards, we look at each other across the table and everything is all right again. I look at him, and if he doesn't know where the sun lives, nothing can convince me that he won't find its address.

He left early this morning and will be gone for a couple of days working on plantations in the southern part of the county. If Mammy was at the plantation, I would go stay with her. She's in Richmond at Master's house there, so I think I will make a new dress for when Forrest takes me riding in the carriage. That'll help him feel free, too.

It is almost dusk when I hear a horse

galloping up the road. I hurry to the door, wondering what Forrest is doing home so soon. It's not him. It's Master.

'Master!' I exclaim, as he gets off his horse.

'Maria,' he says, kind of flat like.

'It sure is good to see you. This is a real surprise. If I had known you were coming, I would've made some of that apple cobbler I know you like.'

He smiles weakly.

'Thank you, Maria. Mind if I come in?'

'Oh, excuse my manners, Master. Come right in, please. Can I get you something to drink?'

He sits down at the table.

'No, thank you.'

I wonder how come he don't want to look at me, but looks over my shoulder and out the door.

'I'm not very good at this sort of thing,' he says, nervously. 'I wish I knew the right way to tell you.'

'What is it? Has something happened to Mammy?' I say, quickly, understanding now. 'You just sit right there, Master. I can be ready to come with you soon as I get my shawl and saddle one of the horses.'

I start out the door.

'It's Forrest,' he says, in a dull voice.

I stop and turn around slowly.

'Forrest?'

'He's dead, Maria.'

I look at him for a moment, then I laugh.

'Dead? No, Master. He just left here this morning. Somebody told you wrong.'

'He went down to the Simpson Plantation, didn't he?'

I nod weakly, the tears coming to my eyes.

'Seems that he was shoeing one of their horses, and Mr Simpson's little boy was watching. He didn't know any better, and he got a stick. He thought it would be funny to watch the horse jump around if he flicked some live coals on it. Forrest was kicked in the head, and died instantly. A boy rode up from there to tell me, and I rode straight out here. I'm sorry, Maria.'

I shake my head and laugh again.

'No, Master. That ain't true. That just ain't true. IT AIN'T TRUE!'

And I run out, past the barn and the corral and into the forest. Then, I cry.

Master sent Mammy to stay with me these weeks since Forrest . . . I still can't say it. How can I believe he's dead when I feel him alive.

I look out the window and see him walking to the barn and exercising the big black horse in the corral. I wake up a half hour before light and start to light the fire in the stove. Then I remember. There's no reason to get up or build a fire or do anything else.

Forrest is laying over there on the other side of the corral, and when it rains, I worry if he's getting wet. There was a frost a few nights ago and I stayed awake worrying about him being cold lying in that ground. Mammy says that it'll be best for me to leave him here, to go someplace where everything won't remind me of him. There ain't no such place. I look at the sky and that reminds me of him. I look at the earth and think of him. I can't go and leave him all alone out there in the ground.

Today Master is coming out from Richmond with Forrest's will. Today I'm free. I wish I wasn't.

It is early afternoon when Master arrives. I was listening for the sound of a horse. He arrives in a carriage and behind him, another white man driving a wagon. I guess it takes more than one white man to read a will.

The long, tall white man in the carriage looks familiar, but I can't place him. Maybe I saw him on the street in Richmond once.

Master doesn't introduce him, but sits down at the table. The long, tall white man stands by the door. Master speaks to Mammy, and barely nods to me. You would almost think he'd come to tell me that Forrest was dead.

He reaches in his coat pocket, and takes out some papers.

'I guess I'll just get right to the point. You understand what this paper is, Maria?'

'Yes, sir, Master. Forrest explained to me about his will and how he was giving me my freedom.'

Master nods.

'That's right. It's all in here. I won't bother to read it to you, because it's all in lawyer's talk. But Forrest gives you your freedom.'

'That's what he told me.'

'There may be a problem, however.'

'What problem, Master?'

'The law says that when a man dies, all the money he owes has to be paid to the people he owes it to. Now, it seems that Forrest owes a fair sum of money.' He unfolds the paper and reads down it until he comes to the part he's looking for. 'He borrowed money from the bank to buy two horses, a carriage, and a ton of oats that was delivered last week.'

'That's right,' I agree.

'Now, what all that means is that you're going to have to pay back all that money.'

'I ain't got no money, Master. You know that.'

'None at all, Maria?'

'No, sir, not unless I sell all the horses, the carriage and the oats.'

'Well, you could sell two of the horses. They're paid for. But the bank that loaned Forrest the money is the real owner of the other two horses, the carriage and the oats.'

I look at him blankly, not understanding.

'I'm sorry, Maria,' Master looks at me sorrowfully. 'I'm afraid that you're going to have to be sold, and the money from that will be used to pay off Forrest's debts.'

'Oh, Master, no!' Mammy exclaims.

'But you just told me the will says I'm to go free.'

'I'm sorry, child. You can't go free if Forrest owes money. All of his property has to be sold to pay his debts. According to the law, you're the most valuable piece of property he owned.'

I remember the other white man now and the way he ripped off the slave girl's dress.

Mammy begins crying.

'Master, you can't let them sell Maria. She's been like a daughter to you. Like a member of your own family.'

She is kneeling beside his chair, her hands clenched almost like she is praying to him. He looks over her and out the window, the colour rising to his cheeks.

'Master! Master!' she sobs. 'Can't you pay off Forrest's debts for her? You got plenty money, Master. You could do that. And Maria, she could come to Richmond and work off the debt to you, and then you could set her free. You could do that, Master! You don't want to see her stood up on the auction block and sold away to somebody who will abuse her. You got too good a heart to do that to her, Master!'

Mammy is sobbing uncontrollably now. I look at Master, waiting to hear what he will say. He looks at me, and his eyes flicker rapidly as if he cannot look at me directly, as if he is afraid to know what he would feel if he looked at me without his eyes fluttering like the wings of a honey bee. Forrest looked at me like that when he was angry and shamed at the same time.

If I ask Master, he'll say yes. That's what

he's waiting for. He did the asking the other time, but he never asked really. I didn't know that I shamed him when I said 'No'. He agreed with me so quickly that I didn't think anymore about it. Maybe he didn't either – until right now. He's got all the power today. If he just says right out that he'll pay Forrest's debts, he won't have the power no more. I will.

I go to Mammy, pulling her from the floor.

'It's all right, Mammy. It's all right. I don't want no new mistress whipping me because she see something in Master's soul he shamed to have there.'

I look at him as I say it, and he drops his head. Suddenly he gets up, gives me a hateful look, and then, with a jerk of his head, tells the slave auctioneer that he can take me. The tall, white man takes a rope from his pocket.

'You don't need to tie me,' I tell him. 'I ain't going to run away.'

And I won't. I can see myself standing up on that platform, and when he tears my dress off, I won't cry. I'll stand up straight, and when the white men start cheering and applauding, I'll stare every one of them in the eye, and make them stop. Won't many of them want to buy me, and whichever one does will wish he hadn't. 'Cos I know. I know now where the sun lives.

Author's note

'Where the Sun Lives' was suggested by the following entry found in Vol. 1 of Helen Catterall's *Judicial Case Concerning Slavery*, p. 210:

William Yates, a free man of colour, died in 1829, having first made his will, by which he gave his whole estate ... to ..., in trust for his wife, Maria, who was his slave, to be paid over to her as soon as she could obtain her freedom, and get permission to remain in the State. All the personal assets were insufficient to pay the testator's debts and Maria was sold.

A Christmas love story

Ellen held the oak-framed oval mirror in front of her and stared. She did not see the smooth, creamy white skin, the grey-green eyes, or the brown hair which fell down her back like a silken waterfall. She looked, instead, at the dark-skinned man standing behind her, his face without a smile or frown.

'I can't do it, William,' she said, lowering the mirror. 'I'm sorry. I can't do it.'

Emotion made her voice even deeper and more husky than normal. William put a hand on her shoulder and squeezed gently.

'I know,' he said, softly. 'I'm afraid, too.'

She turned and looked at him.

'You are?' she asked, surprised.

His admission of fear was oddly comforting. If he had said otherwise, she would have been too alone. She would be alone enough during the next four days. One mistake by her, one false move or word, and they would be caught. William was depending on her.

'I love you, William Craft,' she said, turning round and hugging him to her. 'And if we're both afraid, then we are stronger.'

She released him, and sat down in the straight-back chair in front of the dresser, the mirror in her lap.

'I'm ready, now,' she said.

William began cutting her hair, patiently, snipping an inch away at a time, as if he hated what he was doing.

That straight hair had fooled him into believing she was a white woman the first time he saw her. When he learned she was a slave like himself, he could not believe it, though he should have. He had been a slave in Georgia all of his twenty-four years. It was not uncommon for slave owners to have children by black women. He had seen many, and no matter how white their skins, how grey, green, or light-brown their eyes, or how straight and smooth their hair, William always knew they were slaves like himself.

Why, then, had he not known that Ellen was a slave, too, that July day two years ago? He had looked up from the bureau he was sanding to see her walk slowly past the window. Was it the way she held her head level and steady on her slender neck? Was it the slow, almost leisurely way she had passed the cabinet-maker's shop where he worked? She looked like the favoured daughter of a wealthy planter out strolling, or on her way to have tea at a friend's.

It was almost impossible for a slave not to bear the marks of his or her condition, no matter how much he or she hated it. Shoulders carried proudly would acquire a stoop eventually, and a person's eyes would become furtive, flitting around in their sockets like tiny birds at the approach of a cat. He had seen that look, particularly in the slaves who worked harder than mules on the plantations.

He supposed he had been lucky that his owner hired him out as an apprentice to a cabinetmaker when he was fourteen. After a few years, some of the wealthiest families in Macon were coming to the shop and asking him to make sideboards, tables and bureaus. From the money he earned, two hundred dollars a year went to his owner. He was allowed to keep the remainder.

Having a skill, being paid for his labour, and the basic solitude of his work had kept him secreted from the crushing weight of slavery. Ellen has been spared, too, being a lady's maid and her mistress' favourite servant. She was also her mistress' half-sister.

William clipped more rapidly now. Clumps of soft, fine hair dropped to her lap and on to the floor at his feet. It was as if remembering had rekindled his hatred of being a slave, and he expressed it by removing that hair whose softness he loved to feel beneath his hand, even as he hated the white man who had bequeathed it and hated the grey-green eyes and the white complexion of this woman he adored, this woman who was his wife.

Now he was done. Quickly, he took a clothes brush and whisked the clipped hair from her shoulders and back. Moving around to look at her, he stared for a moment, and taking a comb from the top of the dresser, pushed the hair back.

'There,' he nodded, satisfied. 'Maybe I should have been a barber instead of a cabinet-maker.'

Ellen raised the mirror and looked at herself. She did not think she looked any more like a man than when her hair had hung to her waist. But she was not surprised that she felt relieved to be rid of her father's hair – the hair of the man who had also been her owner and who had never looked at her with any expression other than the frown he bestowed on all his slaves. Ellen was only sorry that William could not also change the colour of her eyes and blacken her skin. But if that were possible, their plan would not work. For the first and only time in her life, she was glad her father had been a white man. At least, she would be glad in four days time – if all went well.

She stood, brushing clumps of hair from her lap.

'You get ready,' William told her. 'I'll sweep.'

Ellen smiled. She still marvelled at William's ability to sweep a floor without raising a wisp of dust. That had been his first job at the cabinetmaker's – sweeping the floor of wood shavings, sawdust, nails and dowels, and doing it without covering the finished and half-finished chairs, tables, and bureaus with dust and debris. How could she *not* have married a man who handled a broom like that, she wondered, laughing to herself. The few times she had ever tried to sweep, you would have been forgiven for thinking a duststorm had gone through the room.

She went behind the screen standing in a corner of the room and began putting on the unfamiliar clothes. Did a man put on his trousers before his shirt, or vice-versa? William put on his pants first, and, for some reason, always the left leg before the right. On one occasion, he had put his right leg in first, stopped, taken it out, and put the left leg in. She chuckled as she slipped her left leg into the pants.

'Well?' she asked, tentatively, when she finally emerged from behind the screen. 'Do I look like a young white southern gentleman?'

William looked at her with a critical eye. The white shirt and dark suit fitted her well, and when her disguise was complete, he believed she would be able to pass for a man. He smiled.

'I think it's going to work, Ellen. I think it's going to work,' he said.

'If it doesn't, we're going to be sold so far into slavery that the Lord won't be able to find us on Judgement Day,' she said, sardonically.

'How do the shoes feel?' he wanted to know.

'Better. I'm glad I practised walking in them the past few nights, but I still don't understand how men ever get anywhere. It's like walking with fish traps strapped to my feet.'

'Good,' he said, absentmindedly, but still

looking at her critically. 'Now, come over here and sit on the bed and I'll finish making you into a cultivated young man on his way to Philadelphia with his man-servant for medical treatment.'

As he took the long swathes of white cloth from beneath the bed, he wondered again if it was an insane idea. It was, and that was its safety. He was glad that it had been Ellen's idea, because everything depended on her. He wrapped swathes of cloth around her right hand and wrist, then pulled it over her shoulder and back, tying it into a sling.

'Is that too tight?' he asked.

She shook her head.

He took the other piece of cloth and wrapped it around her face, covering the smooth and hairless skin which would give her away as a woman, and tied it over her head.

'Where's the hat?'

'Oh, I left it behind the screen.'

William got the hat and placed it on her head. He handed her the mirror.

'Well, what do you think?' he asked.

Ellen gazed at the unfamiliar face in the mirror.

'Well, if nothing else, I certainly look like I'm on death's doorstep.'

William took the black cravat from the dresser and tied it round her neck. Finally, he reached in his coat pocket and handed her the green spectacles. She put them on.

'Your face is almost totally hidden now,' William said, pleased. 'People will see the spectacles and the bandages, but not you.'

She raised the mirror and looked at herself again.

'I hope so,' she said, softly. 'I hope so. These next four days are doing to be worse, I think, than the twenty-two years I've been in slavery.'

'Don't think about it. Just think about being in Philadelphia on Christmas day, and having freedom for a Christmas present.'

'Do I dare, William? Do I dare?'

'If we don't dare, we'll die as slaves.'

She nodded slowly.

'I know. But I couldn't go through with this if it were just for me.'

'Nor I,' he agreed.

'But I will not have children born into slavery!' she flared, suddenly. 'I will not! To have children and see them sold away from us, or us from them, as you saw your mother, father, brother and sister sold. I would kill any child I birthed into slavery.'

William blew out the candle, knowing that a light seen coming from the cabin of slaves at that time of night would arouse suspicion in anyone walking along the street.

They sat on the edge of the bed, neither of them daring to sleep – even if they had been able. No more words were spoken. There was only the waiting now.

The night passed so slowly that Ellen began to wonder if God had commanded the sun not to rise. But when the sky changed from black to inky blue, she did not notice until William touched her arm.

Though the rim of the sun's orb had not yet cleared the horizon, the blue-black of first light quickly changed to a deep ultramarine, and through the window, Ellen could see the shapes of the trees. When the shapes changed to the spare limbs and branches of oak and elm, William squeezed her hand.

'It is time,' he whispered.

Ellen would not release his hand.

'William?' she said, finally, her voice faint.

She turned and stared into his face, and then traced it gently with her fingertips – the eyebrows, the full lips, the thick moustache which still tickled sometimes when they kissed.

'If . . . if something happens and I never

see you again, I want you to know that I love
you more than I have ever been able to say.
Do you know that, William?'

'I know, Ellen. If something does happen,
I'll find you, if not here, then in the life beyond.
But I will find you, wife.'

'I'll be waiting. Forever would not be too
long to wait for you.'

They kissed and held each other for a long
moment before William broke the embrace.

'We must go, or we'll miss the train,' he
said.

He put on his white beaver hat, and took
the two, already packed, valises from beneath
the bed. They walked softly to the door.
William opened it and peered out. All was
still. Even the trees appeared as stolid as
tombstones.

'Come,' he whispered.

Ellen didn't move, as tremors suddenly
shook her body.

'What's wrong?' William asked, sharply.

She burst into tears and put her arms
around his neck, squeezing him so tightly that
it hurt. He dropped the valises, pushed the
door shut, and put his arms around her.

She was glad for his silence, loved him even
more for knowing there were no words that

could quiet the terror attacking her at this moment. There were no words that could reconcile her to the rage she felt at having to, literally, steal their own lives. And if they failed? He would probably be sold to a plantation to work like yoked oxen until he died. And some white man would pay handsomely to use her for his pleasure, as her mother had been used.

Her sobbing stopped almost as suddenly as it began.

'Come, William. It is getting late,' she said, pulling herself together.

He opened the door and they stepped out, as softly as the dawn sending a warm band of red and orange across the eastern horizon. They tiptoed across the yard to the street, afraid that the slightest sound might waken those who slept on the upper floor of the large white house on the corner where her half-sister-mistress lived with her family.

When they reached the sidewalk, William handed her her valise. There was nothing more to say, and as if to acknowledge that they were no longer Ellen and William Craft, but Mr William Johnson and his slave, they turned and walked in opposite directions toward the railroad station.

William walked quickly, afraid he might be recognised by some early riser. He and Ellen had asked for, and been given, four-day passes by their respective owners. It was not unusual for slaves to be given passes at Christmas time to go visiting, so his presence on the street so early would not be questioned. He and Ellen would not be missed even until they were safely in Philadelphia. But he was afraid of being detained for any reason, and was glad when he reached the station and boarded the Negro car where he had to ride.

Ellen walked slowly. She was surprised at the stillness and peace she felt now. Even if they were caught, she had walked across some invisible line, and no one could ever take this moment from her, the first moment in her life when she knew what it was to be free, to be walking along the street early on a quiet and peaceful morning. There was a slight chill in the air, but the sky was clear. The sun would warm the day. That was what it was like to go from slave to free woman. One minute she had been cold. Now she was warm. They could never take that from her.

As she neared the red-brick railroad station, she adjusted her hat and reminded herself that she was now William Johnson. She remembered all the white men she had seen, how they hooked their thumbs in the pockets of their vests, crossed their legs when they sat, flicked invisible bits of lint from coats and trousers with a flick of thumb and forefinger. It was little things like that which identified a man.

As she entered the station, she noticed the line at the ticket-window. As William had predicted, the ticket-seller would have no time for idle talk, or questions. From behind the green spectacles, she looked over the people in the station, afraid there might be someone who would recognise her. There was no one.

'Two for Savannah,' she said, when she got to the window.

The ticket-seller did not look up, but reached beneath the counter, took two tickets, stamped them and shoved them beneath the window grill. She pushed the money toward him and walked away.

William saw her as she emerged from the station. Only when he heard the loud sigh escape his body did he realise how tense he was. Ellen did not look toward the back of the train where the Negro car was, but proceeded slowly along the platform and entered the third car from the front.

William sighed again. Now, if the train

would only start moving. He stared at the people coming on to the platform to say good-bye to friends and relatives. Just then, someone rushed out, pushing and shoving his way through the crowd. William almost leaped from his seat, and his heart pounded as loudly in his ears as the hammer with which he had pounded so many nails.

There, hurrying toward the train was Samuel Ross, the cabinetmaker for whom he worked – a tall, lean man with a sharp nose like a rooster's beak. Ross stopped a white man, speaking rapidly while pointing to the train. The man shook his head, and Ross walked quickly toward the train.

Cursing to himself, William snatched the white beaver hat from his head, and put it on the seat beside him. There were some whites, William knew, who seemed to have some kind of sixth sense about their slaves, and Samuel Ross was one. He hadn't wanted to give William the pass.

'What do you need a pass for?' he had asked. 'You see your wife every night. I could understand if she lived on one of the planta-tions in the countryside.'

'Yes, sir,' William said, seeming to agree. 'That's just it. My wife and I would like to go visit her mother, and since I've never asked for a pass, sir, I didn't think you'd mind this once, sir.'

Though William had kept his eyes looking downward in the proper pose of submission, he could almost feel Ross thinking. White men lived in fear of slaves escaping. Any request a slave made was scrutinised for hidden means of running away.

'Well,' Ross began, finally, 'I better see you bright and early the day after Christmas. If I don't, I'll have the slave-catchers after you so quick you'll wish you'd never been born.'

Now, here he was, entering one of the train's coaches – the one, William realised, where Ellen sat! William waited, scarcely breathing, and though only a moment passed, it seemed like hours before Ross walked off the coach, and hurried to the next one. Just as quickly he was off that coach and leaping up the steps to the next. Two more coaches and he would come to the last one – the Negro coach.

'We are caught,' William mumbled, and angry tears moistened his eyes as he pounded his fist on the coach seat.

But almost in response to the blow, the train jolted, once, twice, a third time, and slowly, began moving. William saw Ross jump from the train, and though he wanted to frame his face in the window for Ross to see, William shrank down in the seat. It was some moments before he dared sit up again.

Ellen has not seen Ross when he entered the car. She was gazing through the window, wondering why, at the moment of leaving, there were these unwanted feelings of sadness. She couldn't believe that she would really miss Rebecca. But why shouldn't she? They were half-sisters, weren't they, and looked so much alike that many white people used to comment to Rebecca's mother about her two lovely daughters. That was why Rebecca's mother had wanted to sell Ellen as far away from Georgia as possible. For some reason, it never happened. Eventually, though, she got rid of Ellen, giving her to Rebecca for a wedding present, as if she were a bowl of cut crystal, or a place setting of silver.

Foolishly, Ellen had expected her half-sister to free her. Instead, Ellen continued to wait on Rebecca as she had since she was seven, and Rebecca, ten. Ellen woke her in the morning, took out her chamberpot, carried warm water from the kitchen for her to wash with, made the bed, laid out her clothes, mended her dresses and underwear, sewed new clothes for her, brushed her hair – as long and as brown as Ellen's – and listened to her chatter. Perhaps it would be about the ball at the Markham Plantation, or dinner with the Bells in Atlanta.

Once a day, Rebecca would hug Ellen.

'Oh, Ellie! You're my dearest friend in all the world! I don't know what I'd do without you!'

Learn to mend your own drawers, Ellen had wanted to tell her so often.

Now, as she felt the train gathering speed, she knew that her sadness had nothing to do with leaving her half-sister who would've sold her if she had ever needed the money. Ellen's sadness was natural, because she was leaving all that was familiar. No matter how right it was to leave, her emotions knew only that they were being carried into the new and the un-known. Afraid, they clawed and clung to the known – no matter how horrible.

When the city of Macon passed from her window to be replaced by the flat, red clay countryside, Ellen turned and was surprised to find that someone had taken the seat next to her. Out of the corner of her eye, she saw something familiar. It appeared to be a walking stick, whose knob was artfully carved into a face, a carved face she had looked at only three nights ago when Mr Cray, a cotton dealer from Savannah, had come for dinner with Rebecca and her husband.

Ellen was afraid she was going to faint, or worse, cry out. Was it just coincidence that Mr Cray was on the same train? But coincidence would not have placed him beside her. How could he have found out? She and William had told no one. Ellen turned to look through the window again, biting her lip to hold back the tears.

'It is a very fine morning, sir,' Ellen heard Cray's rich bass voice say.

Was he addressing her?

'I said, it's a fine morning, isn't it, sir?'

He *was* addressing her.

'I'll make him hear,' Cray said, insulted and annoyed now. 'It's a very fine morning, sir!'

His voice reverberated throughout the coach. Ellen knew she had to do something, but if she turned and he recognised her, it was all over! On the other hand, what if she looked him directly in the eye, spoke, and he saw a man?

She turned her head, and found his eyes

staring into hers.

'Yes, it is a fine morning,' she said. 'I hope you will excuse my hearing.'

She smiled, and turned back to look out of the window again, her heart fluttering as rapidly as the wings of a hummingbird.

'It's a terrible thing to be deaf,' she heard someone behind her whisper to Mr Cray.

'It certainly is,' he returned, sympathetically. 'I won't trouble that young man, anymore.'

Ellen didn't relax, however, until the train stopped at the next town and Mr Cray got off.

It was evening when the train arrived in Savannah. As William put on his white hat and walked off the car, he could smell the ocean. He had never smelled it before, but there was a heavy saltiness to the air. That could only be the ocean, he concluded.

He walked slowly forward to the car where his 'master' was. When 'he' descended the steps, William did not look up into that face he loved so completely, but with one hand, reached for 'his' hand, while taking the suitcase from 'him' with the other. As Ellen stepped onto the station platform, she squeezed William's hand before releasing it.

'Were you able to rest, Master?'

'I'm afraid not, William.'

'Perhaps you'll be able to sleep tonight on the steamer.'

'I hope so.'

The station platform was crowded with disembarking passengers and their friends and family who had come to meet them. It was Christmas time, Ellen reminded herself, a time for reunions and cheeriness. Or so she had observed.

She wondered why William was standing there holding the valises. Then she remembered. She was the master and had to find the carriage to take them to the dock to the steamer for Charleston, South Carolina.

She started slowly across the platform and through the station, William, a discreet two paces behind. Once on the street, a man standing beside a carriage stepped forward quickly.

'Going to the Charleston steamer, sir?'

Ellen nodded, 'Yes'.

'Right this way. That your nigger?'

'Yes, he is. And a more faithful servant cannot be found in all of Georgia.'

The man opened the door of the carriage.

'Well, consider yourself blessed by God,' he said.

'I do,' Ellen responded, smiling to herself as William took her hand and squeezed it tightly as he helped her inside.

'You can ride up top with me, boy,' the carriage driver told William.

As the carriage moved slowly through the streets of Savannah, William wished it had been daylight so he might see something of this city by the ocean. It was a place favoured by many wealthy whites, especially at this time of the year when the weather might turn chilly in central Georgia. He'd overheard whites in the cabinet shop talk of plants and trees growing in this city that must be wondrous to see – palm trees, oak trees with hanging moss. It was odd to be in a place and not know exactly where he was.

If whites had not talked so casually around him at the shop and around Ellen at Rebecca's, as if slaves did not have ears or brains, they would not have known what to do. But, by putting together the conversations they had overheard so many times, they learned how to travel from the south to the north and freedom. At least, he hoped they had.

When they arrived at the wharf, William leaped down and opened the door to assist his 'master'. While he took the valises, Ellen paid the driver. They walked up the gangplank in silence, and William waited nervously while his 'master' bought the tickets. The ship's captain directed the ill-looking white man to his cabin.

Once inside, Ellen threw her free arm around William and they clung to each other for a moment.

'How are you?' William wanted to know.

'Good, I suppose,' she said, weariness in her voice. 'I had a frightful scare, though.'

She told him about her encounter with Mr Cray. William related the sudden appearance of Mr Ross and the train's fortuitous departure before he got to the Negro coach.

'Well, with two narrow escapes like that, do you suppose it could be an omen?' Ellen wanted to know.

'I hope so.'

Ellen sank down onto the bed.

'Could you take the sling off?' she asked.

William shook his head.

'I don't think that's a good idea. What if something happens, and someone comes in the middle of the night and you don't have it on?'

'You're right,' she sighed. 'But my arm is so stiff, I wonder if I will ever have feeling in it again.'

'Once we're in Philadelphia, I'll kiss it back to life,' he said, smiling broadly.

'William Craft!' she exclaimed, laughing and blushing.

'I love you, wife,' he said, kissing her softly. 'Now, it's about time for you to go down to supper, isn't it?'

She shook her head.

'Not tonight, William. I just don't think I could carry off being the young slave owner tonight.'

'But you haven't eaten all day,' he protested.

'I'll be fine,' she reassured him. 'Sleep is what I need.'

'Very well, I'll see you at breakfast.'

'Must you go so soon?'

'It's best not to arouse suspicion.'

She nodded.

'Be careful, husband,' she said.

'I will.'

When William returned to the deck, he was surprised that he could not see the wharf. It took him a moment to realise that the ship was moving. How could that be? To move and not feel the motion. Was this what it felt like to be a white, fluffy cloud against an endless blue sky?

He stood at the rail for a moment, looking out into a black nothingness, which he knew was the ocean. What did it look like? He couldn't imagine water so wide that there was nothing else to be seen. So dark was it, he would have thought he had become a star against the night if he had not been able to see the stars above him.

The breeze carrying the smells of the unseen ocean was chilly now, and just as he was wondering where the coloured passengers slept, the captain came up to him.

'Your master didn't look too well, boy,' he said, roughly.

'No, sir. He sick,' William responded, deliberately using the poor grammar expected of him.

The captain laughed harshly.

'You'd have to be blind not to see that. What's wrong with him?'

'He sick, sir,' William said, grinning. 'I don't know the sickness.'

'Well, I just hope he doesn't die on my boat.'

'Massa die?' William exclaimed, laughing. 'Aw, sir. Massa not gon' die. No, sir! He just don't look so good right now, because of all

114

the travelling. That's all, sir.'

'Hope you're right,' he said, and turned to walk away.

'Begging your pardon, sir?' William called after him.

The captain stopped and turned around.

'What is it?' he asked, roughly.

'Where is the place the niggers sleep at?'

'Boy, you know how to sleep on your feet, don't you? That's all niggers good for, anyway. Sleeping and eating. Ain't no cabins on my boat for niggers.'

He laughed loudly, and walked away.

William walked the deck until he saw a pile of cotton sacks lying near the steamer's funnel. It was warm there and he lay down placing his hat beside him. As tired as he was, he did not sleep, but gazed into the night sky. He remembered when he was a child, before his parents were sold. He remembered the summer nights he had stared up and into the night as he was doing now. It had made him feel he wasn't a slave, but just a little boy wondering why the stars did not fall out of the sky, and wondering if the stars could see him as clearly as he saw them. Did he twinkle in the night to their eyes as they did to his? He remembered wondering, too, why he had been born a slave and not something free, like a star. He wasn't a child any longer, but he still wondered about that.

When the sun rose, he got up and went to the rail to look at the ocean. He was disappointed that it looked scarcely different from a large, wrinkled piece of cloth. Unlike the night sky, which made him wonder about himself and the world, the ocean was simply there. It did not twinkle and brood. It just lay there.

He did not know how much time passed before he heard voices. He walked into the dining hall. Five men were sitting down to breakfast. William moved forward quickly to help his 'master', who was just taking a place next to the captain.

'You seem to be feeling better this morning,' the captain said to Ellen.

'Yes, thank you.'

'I hope your ailment is not serious.'

'I don't think so. My doctor believes it to be an attack of inflammatory rheumatism,' she added, using a term she'd overheard once from one of Rebecca's dinner guests. 'He recommended that I see a physician in Philadelphia.'

Breakfast was served then, and William

leaned over to cut his 'master's' food into small pieces.

'Will there by anything else for now?' William asked.

'No, William.'

As soon as he returned to the deck, the captain spoke.

'You have a very attentive boy, sir. But you had better watch him like a hawk when you reach Philadelphia. I know several gentlemen who have lost valuable niggers in the North.'

Before Ellen could muster a reply, a man sitting opposite with a long moustache that curled downward to the corners of his mouth spoke to her. He had both elbows on the table, a large chicken breast in his hands, and a fair portion in his mouth.

'Good advice, Captain. Very good advice,' he spluttered, dropping the chicken breast into the plate and leaning across the table to stare intently at Ellen. 'I would not take a nigger to the North under any circumstances. I have dealt with many niggers in my time. I never saw one who put his heel upon free soil that didn't either run away or amounted to a hill of beans when he came back to these parts.'

He picked up the piece of chicken, and continued.

'Now, sir, if you wanted to sell that nigger of yours, I'm the man to talk to. Name your price and if it's reasonable, I'll put the silver dollars on the table right this minute.'

The man took a large bite out of the chicken breast, but his eyes did not waver from Ellen's face. She forced herself to meet his gaze, though she felt she was staring into Death's very own face.

'I do not wish to sell, sir,' she said, calmly. 'I cannot get on well without him.'

The man snorted.

'You'll do without him pretty quick if you take him to the North. I have seen lots of niggers in my time, and I guarantee you that that is a keen nigger. I can see from the cut of his eye that he is certain to run away. You'd better sell him to me and let me put him on the market down in New Orleans.'

'I think not, sir,' Ellen responded, firmly. 'I have great confidence in his fidelity.'

'Fi*devil*!' the slave trader exploded, banging his fist on the table and accidentally catching the edge of his saucer sending the cup of hot coffee spilling into the lap of the man seated next to him. The scalded man jumped up with a sudden shriek, only to be patted on the arm by the slave trader.

'Sit down, neighbour,' he said, brusquely. 'Accidents will happen in the best of families.'

Without another glance, he turned back to Ellen, and pointing his finger directly at her, he went on with his speech.

'It makes me mad to hear a man talking about fidelity in niggers,' he said. 'There isn't a one who wouldn't run away, given a chance. If I was President of these United States, I wouldn't let any man take a nigger into the North and bring him back to the South. These are my flat-footed, everyday, right up and down sentiments. I am a Southern man every inch on me to my backbone.'

Suddenly, the men at the table stood.

'Three cheers for the sunny South! Hooray! Hooray! Hooray!' they shouted.

Alone, in the midst of the raucous yells stood a portly, balding man, the front of his trousers wet and stained with coffee. Ellen thought he looked as if he wanted to cry, and when he noticed the 'young gentleman's' look of sympathy, he smiled gratefully.

Just then, someone opened the dining room door, and announced that the steamer was approaching Charleston harbour. The men dispersed, and Ellen returned to the cabin, grateful to find William waiting for her there.

'That was an ordeal!' she exclaimed, after they had embraced.

'The noise had me a little nervous.'

Ellen chuckled.

'Oh, they were worried about your fidelity, William. You aren't going to get up North and fall in love with some fancy Northern girl, are you?'

'What are you talking about?' he asked, bewildered.

Suddenly her body slumped and William held her to him.

'I was just trying to make a joke before I became hysterical,' she said, weakly.

'Three more days,' William whispered.

'Three hundred years would not seem so long.'

Knowing there would be a crowd at the dock, William and Ellen were afraid to disembark immediately. They feared they might be recognised, or that Ross had acted on his suspicion and telegraphed a message for the authorities to be on the lookout for them.

The wharf was practically deserted when they finally left the boat, William holding Ellen by the arm. They took a carriage to the hotel – a hotel which Ellen had heard Rebecca mention as the best in Charleston.

Ellen rested through the day. That evening, she and William returned to the wharf for the next part of their journey.

'A ticket for myself and my slave to Philadelphia, sir,' Ellen told the ticket agent.

The agent's face was the colour and texture of cheese, and he scowled through the grill.

'Boy!' he yelled suddenly at William who stood to the side.

'Sir?' William responded, quickly.

'Do you belong to this gentleman?'

'Yes, sir!'

The agent turned back to Ellen.

'You have to register your name here, sir, the name of your nigger, and pay a dollar duty on him.'

Ellen paid the dollar, then pointed to her bandaged hand.

'As you can see, I am not able to write,' she said.

This was literally true. She was glad now that she had thought of having her arm and hand bandaged. Nothing would have given them away as escaping slaves more quickly than the inability to write. She looked at the agent.

'I would be grateful if you would sign for me, sir,' she told him.

The agent shook his head vigorously.

'I won't do it! No, sir! I won't do it!'

Ellen wondered if he suspected something. Or was he one of those people who enjoyed being contrary? Whatever his motive, it didn't matter. What would she do if he continued to refuse? Would it be something ridiculous like this that would lead to their undoing?

Just then a man with a round, pudgy face and wearing a top hat walked up to Ellen, smiling.

'Having a problem?' he asked warmly, patting Ellen on the back.

For an instant, Ellen was confused. Then she recognised the man on whom the coffee had been spilled that morning. She smiled warmly.

'The ticket agent says I must register my slave, but, as you can see, my infirmity prevents me from writing, and the agent will not do the writing for me.'

'Nonsense!' the man exclaimed, pointing his finger at the ticket agent. 'See here, sir? I know this young man's people. Good family. One of the best in the South. Now, kindly enter his and his slave's name in the register so he might be on his way.'

Ellen couldn't believe what she was hearing. Why was he telling such a lie? Was he that grateful for the look of sympathy she had given him as he stood at the table looking very foolish and alone?

The ticket agent appeared confused now and looked over his shoulder at someone Ellen could not see.

'That's good enough for me, Eli.'

Ellen heard a voice, then saw the captain of the steamer come into view.

'I will register the gentleman's name and take responsibility myself,' he said.

Ellen thanked the captain and her companion from the boat warmly, and William moved forward quickly to assist his 'master' out of the terminal and onto the steamer.

Once the steamer was under way, the captain came to Ellen and explained.

'I hope that you will not take what happened as a sign of disrespect, Mr Johnson. They make it a rule to be very strict in Charleston. I have known families to be detained there with their slaves until reliable information could be received respecting them. You know it would be mighty easy for an abolitionist to come down here, pose as a slave owner and take off a lot of valuable slaves.'

'Yes, you're quite right,' Ellen agreed. 'Quite right. I appreciate your assistance more than I can say.'

William slept fitfully that night, curled in a corner of the deck near the funnel. He woke often during the night, however, concerned not only that they had come close to being caught, but worried even more about Ellen. If his own nerves were frayed, Ellen's must be near to unravelling.

'Only two more days,' he whispered through the night to her. 'Two more days, my love.'

The steamer reached Wilmington, North Carolina, after breakfast the next morning. William and Ellen transferred without incident to the train for Richmond, Virginia.

Ellen settled wearily onto the lumpy train seat. She had thought by now she would be accustomed to her role. But the closer they came to freedom, the more nervous and frightened she was. How much worse to be caught now than at the beginning. And the closer they came, the more she doubted that they would succeed. How could they? How could everyone not see there was a woman behind the bandages and the green spectacles?

But, maybe there was something about her that looked like a man. She wanted to take her mirror from the valise and look at herself closely, to reassure herself that there was something womanly about her. She needed William to tell her how beautiful she was. When these four days were ended, she would want to hear him tell her that for the next 4,000 days, and then make him begin again.

A young woman and a man with a full and neatly trimmed black beard sat down in the seat across from her. The woman looked to be only a year or two younger than Ellen, and with her sparkling blue eyes and cheeks flushed red from the morning chill, she was quite lovely.

Though Ellen didn't want to talk, she found herself in yet another conversation about the bandages and her health. The young woman chattered a little too eagerly, Ellen noticed, her cheeks flushing red long after the chill should have left them. When the young woman, her eyes cast downward, shyly and gravely offered 'Mr Johnson' an apple, Ellen could not help blushing. The girl was attracted to her – or, to 'him', she corrected herself.

Ellen thanked the girl warmly, and didn't know what else to say, embarrassed for herself and the girl. Ellen pleaded fatigue, closed her eyes and pretended to sleep.

After some moments, Ellen heard a deep sigh.

'Papa, Mr Johnson seems to be a very nice young gentleman,' she sighed, again. 'I have never felt so much for a gentleman in my life.'

Ellen was greatly relieved when the train came to the next stop, and she opened her eyes to see the man and his daughter preparing to get off.

The girl's father handed Ellen his card.

'The next time you are travelling this way, Mr Johnson, I would be honoured if you would do us the kindness of calling on us. I would be pleased to see you.' Smiling, he added, 'I believe my daughter would be, too.'

The girl's face turned a deep red.

'Oh, Papa!' she exclaimed, and then, trying to muster her dignity, she looked at 'Mr Johnson' and said solemnly, 'It has been a pleasure meeting you, and I will pray for your health.'

'Thank you,' Ellen said, holding the card in her hand, afraid to cast a glance at it for fear that she might be holding it upside down and would not know.

Only when the man and his daughter had left the train did Ellen put the card in her pocket.

The ride from Richmond, Virginia, to Fredericksburg, Maryland, was quiet, and Ellen slept. At Fredericksburg, she and William transferred without incident to the steamer for Washington DC.

Only two more changes, Ellen thought, as she settled into a chair on the deck. Maybe they were going to make it, after all.

Perhaps she was more optimistic now because, for the first time in three days, she was able to share part of the trip with William. He was leaning against the rail at the other end of the deck. He looked so handsome in his black suit, black cravat, and white beaver hat. When she'd seen it in the store window in Macon, she had insisted he buy it. He had been afraid it would attract too much attention on the trip. She wanted him to dress as handsome as he was, and he was the most wonderful sight she had ever seen.

'Sir!'

The harsh voice was at Ellen's shoulder, and though it startled and frightened her, she willed her body not to tremble.

'I am speaking to you, sir!'

She turned slowly to look into the angry

face of a thin man peering at her through wire-rimmed spectacles.

'Sir?' she responded, with a coolness she didn't feel.

'Is that your nigger?' he asked, pointing at William.

She inclined her head in a curt nod.

'What are you trying to do?' the man sputtered, spittle flecking his lips. 'Spoil him by letting him wear such a fine hat? Just look at the quality of it. The President couldn't wear a better hat. If I had my way, I'd go and kick it overboard.'

A man sitting a few chairs away came over and spoke mildly.

'Come, come, my good fellow. Don't speak in such a way to a gentleman.'

'And why not?' the thin man shouted, his tiny eyes bulging. 'It makes me itch all over, from head to toe, to get hold of every nigger I see dressed like a white man. That nigger ought to be sold to New Orleans and have the devil whipped out of him.'

Ellen rose quickly, but calmly.

'Please excuse me, gentlemen.'

She walked to her cabin, where she fell across the bed, her body trembling, as she bit her lip to hold back the sobs that wanted to escape from her body. There was a knock on the cabin door. She sat up, but was afraid to know who was on the other side. The knock came again.

'Master?'

'Oh, thank God!' she sobbed, hurrying to unlock the door, and admit William. 'Thank God!' she repeated, clinging to him.

'It's almost over,' William said, softly. 'It's almost over.'

When the boat docked at Washington, they transferred quickly to the train for Baltimore, the last major slave port before entering the North.

It was night when the train arrived in Baltimore. The station was crowded with people arriving and leaving, carrying baskets with brightly-wrapped presents.

It was now Christmas Eve, William remembered, but he did not pause to look at the large Christmas tree in the station, its boughs holding tiny lighted candles. He knew that Ellen would not endure much longer. He could feel her body trembling as he guided her through the station and onto the train for Philadelphia. There were too many people around to risk whispering to her, but he squeezed her upper arm tightly as he helped her to a seat.

As he came off the train and made his way to the Negro car, a white-haired man in a gold-braided uniform stopped him.

'Where are you going, boy?' he asked, sternly.

'Philadelphia with my master, sir,' William replied, the quiet calm in his voice hiding the rising fear that something was wrong.

'Where is your master?'

'In the carriage I just left, sir,' William smiled.

'You'd better get him out,' the station master said, firmly. 'And be quick about it! No man can take a slave past Baltimore unless he can prove that he has the right to take him along. Get him off now and bring him to my office.'

William watched the station master walk into the terminal. He didn't know what to do. He had never overheard any slave owner in Macon speak of needing proof of slave ownership to go from the South to the North. Maybe he should quietly disappear now. Ellen would be free, at least, and he would take his chances of finding his own way.

But, if he just disappeared, Ellen would never know what had happened to him. He couldn't do that to her. Slowly, he stepped back on the train and saw Ellen sitting alone at the far end of the coach. She looked up and smiled when she saw him. He managed a weak smile, wondering how he was going to tell her.

'How are you feeling?' he whispered, leaning over the seat.

'Much better.' Her smile was radiant. 'We did it, William.'

'Not quite,' he said, solemnly.

Quickly he told her what had happened.

'No!' Ellen exclaimed loudly, then lowered her voice quickly. 'No, no, no!'

William feared she was going to dissolve into uncontrollable sobbing as she kept repeating, 'No, no, no! No, William! No!'

They were less than twelve hours from Philadelphia and freedom. They couldn't have come so close to be stopped now. Could they?

William grasped her hand.

'Let's go,' he said, gently.

'Go where?' Ellen demanded to know. 'What are we going to do?'

'I don't know. Let's go to the office.'

She gripped his hand fiercely.

'You aren't going to trick me, are you, and run off or do something foolish? I don't want freedom without you, William Craft.'

'No. Let's go to the office. We've come this

far. I just can't believe that we are not meant to go all the way.'

The station master's office was crowded with travellers exchanging holiday greetings with the white-haired man seated behind the large desk at the end of the room. Ellen noticed the bottle of liquor on the edge of the desk, and the glasses of amber-coloured liquid in the hands of the dozen or so men jammed into the tiny room. She noticed, too, that the sounds of joviality diminished as she and William made their way through the crowd. There was only silence when she and William stopped before the station master.

'Did you wish to see me, sir?' she asked, her voice tiny and barely audible to her ears.

'Yes, I did,' the station master said. 'It is against the rules of this railroad, sir, to allow any person to take a slave out of Baltimore and into Philadelphia, unless he can satisfy us that he has a right to take him along.'

Ellen looked at the station master, at the white hair and pale blue eyes that looked at her kindly. He was just an old man doing his job, anxious for the train to leave so he could get home to spend Christmas Eve with his family. There wouldn't be any problem, she was sure. Her voice was strong when she spoke.

'And why is that, sir? Isn't the word of a white gentleman worth anything in Baltimore?' she asked, indignantly.

The pale, soft eyes of the station master hardened so quickly that Ellen was startled, and when he spoke, his voice was so cold, Ellen could feel the warmth leaving her body. She had made a mistake, one which could be fatal.

'Sir, a gentleman would not question the rules of this railroad or the laws of this great city. But if you are so dense that you don't understand, let me explain. If we allowed any gentleman to take a slave past here into Philadelphia, and should the gentleman not be that slave's rightful owner, and should the lawful owner come prove that his slave escaped on our railway, the railroad would have to pay that man what he said his slave was worth. And that money would come out of my pocket! Now do you understand?' he asked, with sarcastic finality.

Ellen felt the eyes of everyone in the room on her. Suddenly there was the sound of a chuckle.

'Now, now, Arnold,' someone said to the stationmaster. 'That's not the proper Christmas spirit, is it?'

'Hear, hear,' came another voice. 'Arnold, you can plainly see the state of the gentleman's health. A gentleman in his condition needs his faithful servant.'

'Furthermore,' came a third voice, 'you don't really think a nigger would try to run away by riding the train, do you?'

Everyone laughed at such a ridiculous idea.

'All I know,' countered the station master, 'is that if a nigger escapes on one of my trains, the railroad would hold me responsible. A nigger like that one there probably goes for a thousand dollars. And that's a thousand dollars I don't have.'

It was an argument none of the men could refute.

'Sir,' one of the men said, addressing Ellen, 'isn't there someone in Baltimore who can vouch for you and your slave?'

'No. I am a stranger passing through to seek medical treatment in Philadelphia,' Ellen said, looking at the station master, who was pouring himself another drink. 'Sir, I bought tickets in Charleston to pass us through to Philadelphia. Therefore you have no right to detain me here. None whatsoever!'

The words were not out of her mouth before she knew she had made another mistake. But she hadn't got this close to be stopped! The man had to be made to change his mind.

The station master leaped up from behind the desk.

'Right or no right! I will not let you pass!' he shouted, his face flushing red, his arm trembling as he pointed at her and shouted even louder. 'I will not let you pass!'

Everyone in the room seemed frozen. No one moved or spoke or even dared breathe it seemed. Ellen knew that she was supposed to turn and walk out. She would have—had she been able to. But she couldn't move. To turn and walk out was the end.

So she stood and stared at the station master. He stared back. Leave, she told herself. Leave. There might be another way to Philadelphia. Maybe William was right. She could go ahead and once in Philadelphia, find some means to locate him and help him escape.

If she didn't walk out soon, the station master would summon the police to eject her, and maybe, arrest her even. And that would be the worst thing that could happen. Leave!

But she could not move. The only sound in the room was the tick-tick of the pendulum of the tall clock behind the station master's desk.

The door of the office opened. Certain that the police had been summoned somehow, Ellen turned. But she had scarcely moved before she noticed that it was only the conductor who'd been on the train from Washington to Baltimore. The conductor sauntered in, and laughed when he saw the bottle sitting on the station master's desk.

'Just the thing I was looking for, Arnold,' he said, brightly.

'Did these two ride in with you from Washington?' the station master asked abruptly, pointing to Ellen and William.

Someone handed the conductor an empty glass and he poured himself a drink. He turned and looked at Ellen and William.

'Those two?' he asked, swallowing the drink quickly, chuckling and wiping his mouth with the back of his hand. 'Now, that'll keep me warm for a while.'

He set the glass on the desk and nodded at Ellen and William.

'Came in from Washington same as I did,' he said. 'Come all the way from Macon, Georgia, believe he said. Going to Philadelphia to see some doctor up there.'

Just then the bell rang, announcing that it was time for the train to leave.

'Well, time for me to go to work,' the conductor said. 'Merry Christmas, everyone.'

'Merry Christmas,' various ones called out, their minds not on Christmas at that moment but the scene in the office.

As the conductor left, the station master threw up his arms and let them fall to his sides.

'I don't know what to do,' he said, his voice soft now. He looked at Ellen and shrugged. 'I suppose it is all right. Since you are not well, it would be a pity to stop you here.'

A great cheer went up in the room.

'That's the spirit, Arnold!'

'I knew you were a good man!'

Quickly the office emptied as the men hurried to board the train, many patting Ellen on the shoulder and back as they left.

'You better hurry,' the station master said to Ellen. 'That train isn't going to wait for you.'

'Thank you, sir,' Ellen said, warmly. 'You'll never know how deeply grateful I am.'

Ellen was the centre of much attention on the train. She didn't know how she managed to smile, laugh, and make conversation. She was empty now, and drained by the terror of

137

these four days minus twelve hours that she feared she might laugh at some harmless remark and, unable to sleep, her laughter would tumble over and down into hysterical sobbing.

'You look a little pale,' someone observed.

'I am somewhat weary.'

'Well, we'll let you rest now.'

'You're very thoughtful.'

Ellen went almost immediately into a sound sleep and was startled to hear a voice.

'Wake up. Wake up.'

'What is it?' she asked, too loudly, afraid that the station master had changed his mind and she was being ordered off the train.

'You have to get off, sir.'

She looked into the conductor's face, panic threatening her sanity.

'Is something wrong?'

'No, no,' the conductor said. 'We're at Havre de Grace. We have to ferry across the Susquehanna River. For the safety of the passengers, we ask them to ride on the ferry itself rather than remain in the coaches.'

It was dark and cold when she stepped outside. A fine mist was falling, which chilled her quickly. She looked around for William who always came to her whenever the train stopped. Ellen had never needed him as she did now, as she felt the ferry move into the cold, misty blackness of the river.

This wasn't like him. Where was he? She could make out the passengers in the light from the lanterns hanging along the ferry railing. He wasn't there! William was not there! He had been caught! She knew it!

She hurried around the ferry until she found the conductor.

'Have you seen my servant, sir?'

The conductor chuckled.

'Oh, he's probably run off and is in Philadelphia by now.'

Ellen ignored his remark.

'Could you find him for me?' she commanded.

The conductor was indignant.

'I'm no slave hunter! If I had my way, every slave in the South would go free tomorrow. You'll get no help or sympathy from me!'

When the ferry stopped on the other side of the river, Ellen had not found William. She wondered if she should board the train, or stay and see if she could learn what had happened to him.

She knew, however, that if he had been

captured, his only solace would be knowing she was free. Reluctantly, she got on the train. She was grateful for the darkness that hid the tears flowing down her face.

She didn't know that she had fallen asleep or how long she had been asleep when a voice awakened her.

'Master?'

Her eyes opened quickly to see William bending over her.

'Oh, William!' she exclaimed, in a hushed whisper. 'Where were you? I thought you . . . '

He put a finger to her lips to silence her, then smiled sheepishly.

'I fell asleep. The conductor didn't bother to wake me when we came to the ferry. I woke up a few minutes ago, and he told me that he'd told you I'd run away.'

Tears flowed down her face again, but these were of relief. In the darkness she found his hand and squeezed it so tightly that he winced.

'It won't be long now,' he told her.

When he returned to the Negro car, the conductor came in, chuckling.

'Your master feel better now?'

'Yes, sir.'

'Well, let me give you some advice, boy.

When you get to Philadelphia, run away and leave that cripple and have your freedom.'

'No, sir,' William said, indifferently. 'I can't do that, sir.'

'Why not?' the conductor wanted to know, surprised. 'Don't you want to be free?'

'Massa good to nigger, sir. Massa good massa him.'

The conductor was outraged.

'Well, of all the dumb things I've heard in my life,' he said before storming out of the car.

William was sorry that he could not tell the conductor the truth. He seemed like a good man, but one could never tell.

'That was good advice he gave you,' William heard a voice say.

He looked around to see a black man seated across the aisle.

'Oh,' William said, noncommittally, hiding his eagerness to talk to this well-dressed black, who by the erect way he sat showed that he had never lived a day in slavery.

'I be better off with massa than free nigger any day,' William said, hoping the man would take the bait.

The free black needed to hear no more to begin telling William about the black churches, fraternal organisations, business, and social life among the blacks in Philadelphia.

'Why there are blacks and whites eager to help someone like yourself escape from slavery.'

He gave William the name and address of a white man who had helped many runaway slaves.

William listened intently, remembering everything he heard. When the man finished, his face awaited eagerly William's response.

'Massa he good massa to nigger,' William said. 'Me and massa grow up like brothers, me and massa did.'

The free black got up in disgust.

'You've got as much sense as a brick.'

He moved to the other end of the coach to be as far away from William as possible. William regretted that the man would never know the truth, or how helpful he had been. But they were too close to take any unnecessary risks.

William drifted off to sleep, repeating the name and address of the white man over and over.

When the shrill whistle of the train awakened him, William opened his eyes and there, through the window, at the beginning of a day as grey as pewter, he saw the buildings of a large city. Philadelphia!

The train had scarcely slowed to a stop before he was out of the coach and hurrying to Ellen. Quickly, they found a carriage, and were driving through the streets of the still city.

William put his arms around Ellen, and she began to cry. It was over, and she could cry now. Her body heaved with the force of the tears, as if the demons of fear and doubt were being torn from her body. She cried, and William held her as if she were a child.

When the carriage stopped at the address, Ellen was so weak that William lifted her from the carriage. Through her tears, she smiled, the green spectacles on her nose looking ridiculous now.

'Merry Christmas, husband,' she said, feeling light in his arms, her arms around his neck.

Then she took the spectacles from her nose and tossed them high into the air.

'Merry Christmas!' she shouted. 'Merry Christmas, everybody!'

And she did not know her laughter from her crying and the tears on her face shone like a smile.

Author's note

'A Christmas Love Story' is the mere beginning of a remarkable, true story recounted in *Running A Thousand Miles for Freedom; or, The Escape of William and Ellen Craft From Slavery* by William Craft. All the incidents in 'A Christmas Love Story' are true.

The Crafts' amazing story continues with them settling in Boston, Massachusetts, where slave hunters eventually located them. Though the abolitionists of Boston forced the slave hunters to leave, threatening them with death, President Millard Fillmore ordered troops to Boston to arrest William and Ellen. They fled to England, where they lived for a time at 12 Cambridge Road, Hammersmith, London. It was there that William wrote the story of their escape.

They returned to the United States in 1868 to head an agricultural school in Savannah, Georgia. The school was burned by the Ku Klux Klan in 1871 and rebuilt in 1873. William and Ellen left in 1878 and returned to live in Boston. My research has been unable to trace them from that point.

Their story does not end there, however. In 1961, I moved from Nashville, Tennessee, to New York City. During my first months in New York I met a young black woman with sandy brown hair, blue-green eyes, and an irrepresible spirit named

Peggy Damon. One day I was sharing with her my feelings of elation at no longer living in the South. 'I think I feel the way William and Ellen Craft must have felt,' I said, for some reason.

She looked at me quizzically.

'What do you know about them?' she asked.

I told her the story of their escape, though I don't recall now where or when I had first heard or read it. When I finished, I asked her, 'Why do you ask?'

She smiled then.

'Oh, I was just curious. William and Ellen Craft were my great-grandparents.'